Harlequin Presents...

Other titles by
ANNE MATHER
IN HARLEQUIN PRESENTS

Many of these titles, and other titles in the
Harlequin Romance series, are available at your
local bookseller, or through the Harlequin Reader
Service. For a free catalogue listing all available
Harlequin Presents titles and Harlequin Romances,
send your name and address to:

HARLEQUIN READER SERVICE,
M.P.O. Box 707
Niagara Falls, N.Y. 14302
Canadian address:
Stratford, Ontario, Canada N5A 6W4
or use order coupon at back of books.

ANNE MATHER

the sanchez tradition

Harlequin Books

TORONTO • LONDON • NEW YORK • AMSTERDAM • SYDNEY • WINNIPEG

© Anne Mather 1971

Original hard cover edition published in 1971
by Mills & Boon Limited, 17 - 19 Foley Street,
London W1A 1DR, England.

SBN 373-70508-5
Harlequin Presents edition published June 1973

Second printing June 1973
Third printing August 1973
Fourth printing November 1973
Fifth printing July 1974
Sixth printing August 1974
Seventh printing April 1976
Eighth printing June 1976

Printed in Canada.

CHAPTER ONE

THE casino at Pointe St. Auguste stood on the promontory overlooking the jagged rocks which had once earned the point its dangerous reputation. That there was little chance now of some craft foundering on the rocks below the point had not dispelled its air of mystery and allure, and the casino was a highly popular night spot for tourists from Nassau only a few miles away. There was a restaurant adjoining the casino which seemed actually poised above the precipice and it was not inconceivable that a loser might consider ending his life by a leap from the balcony rails. Many people came to gamble nightly, and while there might be any number of losers, it was the winners who attracted the attention.

Rachel sat alone at her table in the restaurant at the head of the flight of stairs which led down into the casino proper. From here, she had an advantageous view of the whole gambling area, and her eyes flickered almost cynically over the fabulously jewelled female who was presently extolling her fortunes at the roulette table to the whole company. That she had won was obvious, but her naïve excitement was so unnecessary when she so obviously did not need the money.

Rachel looked away from the chattering throng, studying the amber liquid in her glass with intensity. Would this wealthy patron arouse any interest from the management? She opened her sequined evening bag and produced her cigarette case, placing a cigarette between her lips. But before she had time to flick her lighter a waiter forestalled her, holding a flame to the tip of her cigarette with smiling dexterity. Rachel acknowledged the gesture with a slight smile, glad at least that it was not the young man who had endeavoured to thrust his company upon her earlier in the evening. Sitting alone in a place like this was inviting trouble, she supposed almost wearily, but during the course of the last three days she had spent time alone in much less salubrious surroundings in an effort to achieve her objective.

She looked about her. Everywhere there was evidence of the power that money emanated, and it was depressing to speculate on the waste of it all. Here she was, sitting above an enormous casino, without any intention of joining the tables, yet embarked upon the biggest gamble of her life. She drew deeply on her cigarette. *He* must come here tonight, she told herself passionately. Her funds were running desperately low and she could not, she *would not*, return to England without even having seen him. What would she tell her father if she was forced to do just that? Would he secretly believe she had funked the whole thing? Could he have done any better in her place? She cupped her chin on one slim hand and drew imaginary circles on the polished surface of the table with the other. Could he have done any *worse*?

But it hadn't been easy, she had to justify herself. You couldn't just arrive in an area like the Bahamas and expect to find one man in the space of a few hours, even if that man was well known and affluent. There were over seven hundred islands in the group scattered over some ninety thousand square miles of the south Atlantic. He could have been anywhere. He might even have been in London. It was not impossible. She knew he visited there occasionally. After all, hadn't she met him on just such a visit? She supposed it had been foolish to imagine he would still own the house on the out-island, Conchera, but at least a telephone call had taken care of that and she had not wasted precious time and money chartering a boat to go to the island. He no longer had any part of the hotel to the west of Nassau above that marvellous beach where once they had used to swim, and he had sold the restaurant on Bay Street. Everywhere, she had seemed to draw a blank, and if people knew his whereabouts they were not saying. Of course, using her unmarried name of Jardin she had not aroused any interest or curiosity, and very likely those people she had asked had presumed her to be some kind of crank. It was logical at that. Someone who knew him and who he wanted to know would know of his whereabouts. But she couldn't bring herself to use any other name. She had no intention of giving him the advantage of being forewarned of her presence in Nassau. Maybe that was a foolish and prideful thing to do, but she couldn't help it.

And then, after spending hours in the Tourist Information Office, reading lists of hotels and night clubs, she had happened upon this place. It was the location that had done it. Years ago, he had told her that St. Auguste's Point would make a marvellous site for a night club, and although then he had made no enquiries into its ownership, it was something he might have done in later years. Further enquiries had produced definite proof of ownership, and the head of the syndicate was the man she wanted to see.

She stubbed out her cigarette in the conch shell that served as an ashtray, and swallowed the remainder of her drink. It seemed obvious that it would take more than someone's minor eruption at the tables to attract the attention of the club's management. She frowned. There was nothing for it. She would have to go to the manager's office and ask the whereabouts of the man she wanted to see. It was now or never. She might not get another opportunity. After all, it cost money just sitting here, drinking ginger sodas. And already the waiter was watching her with a speculative gaze. Maybe he thought she was some kind of confidence trickster, or possibly simply a thief. And if she were, there was certainly plenty of game here tonight. The earrings the girl was wearing on the adjoining table must be worth somewhere in the region of five thousand pounds, and the necklace that matched them was incalculable. She glanced down at the only ornamentation she wore, a broad gold band on her forearm. It was plain, but at least it was real, the only piece of jewellery she had retained. Her gown, however, could not compare with any of the creations worn here tonight. It was no Paris model, nor was it richly encrusted with jewels, but its plainness gave it an attraction she was unaware of amongst so many peacock plumes. And the smooth sweep of light chestnut hair was thick and shining, and she looked very young to be in such an adult place.

A man who had been watching her for several minutes unbeknown to her from the vantage point behind a trellis-work of climbing plants nodded decisively to the waiter who had drawn his attention to her and advanced towards her table. Reaching her side, he said in a low voice: 'Are you waiting for someone, madam?'

Rachel looked up, and her eyes darkened with slight impatience. The man's face reflected his absolute astonishment, and he drew out the chair opposite and sat down almost compulsively.

'Rachel!' he exclaimed. 'What are you doing here?'

Rachel linked and unlinked her fingers. At last a familiar face, she thought with relief, and yet also with a feeling of disappointment, for now *he* would learn of her presence with or without her volition.

'Hello, Ramon,' she said, managing a smile. 'How are you?'

'I'm fine, fine!' Ramon Sanchez was impatient. 'I asked—what are you doing here? Does André know you are here?' Then he smote a fist into the palm of his other hand. 'Of course he does not, or I should have known!'

Rachel waited for the brilliance to die out of his eyes, and shrugged her shoulders slowly. 'Your brother doesn't know everything, Ramon.'

Ramon leaned forward. 'Obviously not, but he has only yesterday returned from New York. How long are you here?'

Rachel managed to maintain a cool front. 'Do you mean how long have I been here, or how long am I staying?' she queried calmly.

Ramon chewed his lower lip. 'Both.'

Rachel smiled. 'You're as impulsive as ever, Ramon. Tell me, is it by chance you're here, or do you work here?'

'The casino is my concern,' replied Ramon reluctantly. 'I am here most nights. I will be honest. My man, Arnoux, he noticed you here earlier, and he has been keeping an eye on you.'

Rachel gave a short laugh. 'A suspicious character, is that it?'

'Something like that,' Ramon admitted. 'But necessary, you must agree. One cannot be too careful.'

'No, one cannot,' she agreed, rather dryly.

Ramon rose abruptly to his feet. 'Come,' he said. 'We cannot talk here. We will go to my suite.'

Rachel looked up at him lazily. 'What have we to talk about?'

'André.'

Rachel's cheeks coloured slightly. 'It's André I wish to see.'

'I know that.'

Rachel frowned. 'Is it inconceivable to a member of the Sanchez family that I should be in New Providence for any other reason than to see your brother?' Her tone was harsh.

Ramon bent, resting his hands on the table. 'Yes,' he said bleakly. 'At this time—yes.'

'At this time?' Rachel's frown deepened. 'What does that mean?'

'Do not pretend to be naïve with me, Rachel. Come: I insist. We cannot talk here.'

'And if I refuse?'

'Then you will never see André!'

Rachel compressed her lips. She knew better than to doubt his word, and this might be her last chance to achieve what she came for. With a resigned sigh, she rose to her feet, gathering her gloves and purse. 'Very well,' she said, 'I'll come with you.'

Ramon's eyes narrowed. 'I rather thought you might,' he remarked.

They descended the steps into the casino, the brilliance of its lights contrasting sharply with the intimate lighting of the restaurant. The noise was terrific, and Rachel wondered how the players managed to hear what was going on. Trays of champagne cocktails and heavier spirits were being carried about, and the atmosphere was filled with the scent of perfume and cigar smoke. The thick carpet underfoot was embedded with stubs of cigarettes and cigars, and she wondered how often new carpets were laid. From the opulent appearance of the place it must be redecorated every couple of months or so.

At the far side of the hall was a door marked 'Private' and Ramon unlocked it with some keys from his pocket, nodding casually to the two men who stood, one to either side like bodyguards. Rachel shivered. She rememberd the bars of this gold cage so well.

Inside the office the furnishings were equally as opulent. There was a plentiful supply of drinks on a cabinet, and a positive network of telephones on the wide desk. Ramon crossed to the drinks cabinet and poured her a drink, but she shook her head when he offered her the glass and accepted a cigarette instead. Ramon poured himself a drink, and then walked behind the desk and stood, regarding her intently.

'Won't you sit down?' he requested, nodding to a comfortable chair, and as her legs felt slightly shaky, she did as he suggested. When he was seated too, he said: 'You're looking very beautiful, Rachel. But you don't need me to tell you that.'

Rachel bent her head. 'Where is André?' she asked blankly.

Ramon shrugged, and lay back in his chair. 'What have you been doing with yourself—all these years?'

Rachel compressed her lips. 'Where is André?' she repeated quietly.

Ramon swallowed half his drink and looked deep into his glass. 'He won't see you, you know,' he said chillingly.

Rachel looked up. 'Shall we let him decide?' she asked shortly.

Ramon finished his drink, and getting to his feet walked over to the cabinet again. Rachel's eyes followed him. He was so calm, so aloof, so different from the exuberant young man she remembered. He wasn't much like André really. He was shorter, broader, and younger, of course. During the past five years he had shed that air of youthfulness, and now, at thirty, he was poised and assured. But then all the Sanchez family were poised and assured. It was a family resemblance, and *en masse* it could be destructive.

'Tell me, Ramon,' she said at last, as he poured himself another drink, 'what did you mean when you averred you knew I was in Nassau to see André?'

Ramon turned and came back to his seat. 'You had his letter?'

'His letter?' she echoed incomprehensively.

'The letter from his solicitors, then,' amended Ramon.

'I've had no letter!' exclaimed Rachel, shaking her head. 'No—no letter at all.' She frowned. 'What was in this letter?'

Ramon looked sceptical. 'You don't know?'

Rachel clenched her fists. 'If I did, would I be asking?'

'You might. You might have thought of some clever ploy to thwart André's plans!'

'Plans? What plans?' Rachel got to her feet. 'I tell you I don't know what you're talking about, Ramon. I wish I did. At least if I'd had a letter from him—or his solicitors—I would have known where to find him.'

'I doubt it. André's whereabouts are not for publication.'

Rachel drew herself up to her full height of five feet six, and gripped her purse tightly. 'I'll ask you for the last time, Ramon. What is this all about?'

Ramon chewed his lip, studying her thoughtfully, as though trying to decide whether or not to believe her. Then he lifted his shoulders and said: 'Sit down, Rachel.'

Rachel shook her head. 'I prefer to stand, thank you.'

'Oh, for heaven's sake, sit down,' he snapped. 'All right, all right, so you've had no letter. Why are you here?'

'That's my business!'

'You're not prepared to tell me?'

'No. It's a private matter I want to discuss with André.'

Ramon heaved a sigh. 'I doubt very much whether André will see you, whether he believes you received his letter or not,' he replied. 'He's finally gotten you out of his system. I don't think he will wish to admit you even to his thoughts again.'

Rachel's colour deepened. 'What is that supposed to mean?'

Ramon smote his fist on the table. 'Don't play the

innocent with me, Rachel. Five years ago my brother wanted to *kill* you!'

Rachel shivered again. 'But he didn't!'

'No, but he damn near killed himself!' muttered Ramon furiously. 'God, what am I doing, sitting here talking with you? I ought to just have you ejected from the club!'

Rachel shook her head. 'I still want to see André!'

Ramon got to his feet. 'All right, I'll tell him you're here. Where are you staying?'

Rachel ran her tongue over her dry lips. 'Couldn't I see him tonight? It's—it's rather urgent!'

Ramon stared at her. 'No. No chance!'

Rachel twisted her fingers together. 'Couldn't you make a concession?' she exclaimed bitterly. 'You don't know what happened five years ago, you only think you do! And I have feelings, too, you know!'

'Feelings? Feelings?' Ramon was harsh. 'You don't know the meaning of the word!'

'I do—I do!' Rachel's voice almost broke on a sob, but she fought it back. 'All right, warn your big brother—tell him I'm here! Give him time to put extra bodyguards about him! I don't care! Just so long as I get to see him!'

Ramon reached for a cigar from the box on the desk. 'I can't promise anything. Whatever you're here for, this is the wrong time to choose.'

Rachel suddenly remembered the solicitor's letter. 'The letter?' she questioned. 'What was in it?'

Ramon lit his cigar with deliberation. 'Can't you guess?'

A chill invaded her bones. 'Not—not—a *divorce*?' she asked, almost knowing then that the question was

14

unnecessary.

'How astute you are!' he mocked coldly. 'Now do you see how hopeless your chances are?'

She turned away, breathing swiftly. This was something she had grown out of the habit of considering. Five years ago it had seemed a possibility, a very real possibility, but as the years passed and there was no word, she had begun to accept her strange marriage as lasting. The money had always been there, the first of the month on the dot, and if there had been no communication except through solicitors, she had accepted that, too. She had had her dreams, of course, and in all honesty she had acquired a kind of unsatisfied curiosity about him, but so long as the ties were there, a thread of contact had remained to strengthen her. She didn't know what she had expected to happen in the years to come. Perhaps she had imagined circumstances could alter drastically, but now, faced with the blankness of Ramon's statement, she felt bereft, desolate, and utterly alone.

She gripped the back of the chair for support, her mind buzzing with the complications this could instigate. Her task was made doubly difficult, and doubly humiliating.

'Are you all right?' Ramon had come round the desk to join her, looking at her anxiously. 'You really didn't know, did you?'

Rachel shook her head, not trusting herself to speak, and Ramon released her cold fingers from the back of the chair, and put her into it instead. Then he walked across to the cabinet and mixed her a drink, bringing it back and putting it firmly into her chilled fingers. 'Go on,' he said commandingly. 'Drink it!'

Rachel raised the glass to her lips. It was brandy and the raw spirit caught her throat, causing her to cough convulsively for a moment. Then she recovered and sipped a little more, silently. Ramon studied her thoughtfully, and then when she had finished the drink took the glass from her. Replacing it on the tray, he said: 'Do you feel better now?'

Rachel looked up, a little of the colour returning to her pale cheeks. 'Thank you,' she said quietly.

Ramon uttered an exclamation and went down on his haunches beside her, taking one of her cold little hands in two of his and warming it gently. 'Oh, Rachel,' he murmured huskily, 'what am I going to do with you?'

Rachel's green eyes slanted a little mischievously. This was the Ramon she had known so well and with whom she had shared so many happy hours, escaping from the bars that bound her inside that golden cage.

'What would you like to do with me?' she asked teasingly. 'Drop me over the balcony rails on to the rocks below?'

Ramon shook his head impatiently, bending his mouth to her palm even as an outer door opened without warning and a man and a woman came into the room. Immediately Ramon straightened, dropping Rachel's hand like a hot coal as his eyes met those of the man who had just entered.

Rachel's eyes widened, too, and the colour drained from her face for a second time. With or without Ramon's assistance, she had met André Sanchez at last.

There was absolute silence in the room for several seconds, all of which seemed like aeons to Rachel and during the space of those few seconds she looked again on the man who was her husband and whom she had not seen for the past five years. André Sanchez was all she remembered him to be and more, tall and lean and dark and painfully attractive. His tanned skin was darkened further by the long sideburns he wore, and the ravens-wing blackness of his hair lay thick and smooth against his well-shaped head. He was perhaps thinner than she remembered and at forty years of age there were several strands of grey amongst the darkness at his temples. But physically he looked years younger, the dinner suit he was wearing with such ease and assurance accentuating his leanness. His eyes were the only light thing about him, being of a particularly clear shade of blue, while lines etched either side of his mouth drew attention to the sensual curve of his lower lip. Rachel felt a quiver of awareness run through her body, and a sense of incredulity that she should ever have dared to defy this man. He appeared so arrogant, so invincible; so much the master of his fate.

Ramon spoke first as Rachel's eyes moved to the woman who accompanied her husband. She was tall, too, taller than Rachel, with classically styled hair, and thin aristocratic features. Dressed in a chiffon evening gown that swathed her slender body closely, she was every inch his counterpart, and Rachel could not wholly dispel the sense of antagonism the woman roused in her. There was possession in the way she clung to André's arm, and intimacy in the glances she bestowed upon him. But now Rachel looked at her brother-in-law as he said, rather uncomfortably: 'I didn't expect you to come here this evening, André!'

André Sanchez released himself from his companion's caressing fingers, and moved into the room.

'Obviously not,' he observed contemptuously, his eyes running over Rachel with chilling intensity. Any shocking impact her presence here might have had upon him had been immediately disguised, if indeed there had been any, and no one could tell from his indifferent observation that he was in any way perturbed by this unexpected turn of events.

Ramon gave the woman behind his brother an apologetic smile, and said: 'Good evening, Leonie. I'm sorry about all this.'

The woman called Leonie moved forward, a frown marring her perfect features. 'But what is all this, Ramon?' she enquired, in a husky voice. 'I do not understand. André? Do you know this woman?' She looked at Rachel with appraising eyes. 'Is that why you are all acting like statues newly come to life?'

André Sanchez thrust his hands into the pockets of his dinner jacket and stepped to one side of her. 'I am sorry, Leonie,' he said, rather grimly. 'It was not my intention to create this situation. However, as my brother has seen fit to acquaint himself once again with my wife, I must introduce you.'

'Your wife!' echoed Leonie, a trifle sceptically. 'You cannot be serious, André!'

'It's not what you think, André!' began Ramon protestingly, but Rachel was chilled once again by the look André turned in his brother's direction.

'Leonie, this is Rachel—my wife!' he said bleakly, and Rachel wondered rather wildly whether she was expected to shake hands. But fortunately, Leonie made no such gesture and instead looked up at André appealingly.

'But why is she here?' she demanded. 'You told me

you had already contacted your solicitors!'

'So I have,' replied André, glancing in Rachel's direction. 'It may be that their instructions were not explicit enough.'

Rachel had had enough of this suddenly. The numbness she had felt when she first encountered André Sanchez's icy blue gaze was beginning to wear off, and anger was rapidly taking its place. Everyone was acting as though she were a deaf-and-dumb spectator to their theatrical production. No one had seen fit to address a single word to her, and in addition André was acting as though her presence here was beneath contempt. He had not even had the decency to introduce her to the woman who was to be his wife. What right had he to treat her so diabolically? They were not divorced yet! The agony of it all was that when she looked at him she didn't remember the bad times at all, only the good, and memories could tear her apart.

With a stifled exclamation, she brushed past all of them, making for the door, aware that she was destroying any chance she might have had of making André see reason for her father's sake. All she wanted was escape; escape from the coldness of André's eyes, escape from the compassion in Ramon's, escape from the pitying disdain in Leonie's.

But as she passed her husband, his hand shot out and caught her wrist in a cruel grasp, preventing her headlong flight, and bringing her closer to the bleakness of his face. 'A moment, Rachel,' he murmured harshly. 'Do not imagine you can make a fool of me and get away with it a second time!'

Rachel glared at him, aware that she was fighting back stupid emotionalism as tears burned the back of her eyes. 'Don't touch me!' she cried bitterly. 'Let me get out of here!'

André shook his head slowly. 'I think not. At least—not until I know how and why you are here, and what lies you have been telling my brother.'

Rachel's hand stung across his cheek before he could prevent it, but he still did not release her wrist, tightening his grip so that she felt the blood drain away. She could not see Ramon's expression, he was behind her, but the woman, Leonie, stared at her in disgust. 'André darling——' she began, touching his arm appealingly, but André's attention was centred, for the moment, on Rachel.

'Still the same old Rachel!' he snarled. 'Did you enjoy doing that? Do you know how near I came to returning the compliment?'

Rachel trembled. 'Oh, let me go! God, I was a fool to come here!'

'I would agree with you there,' he commented savagely. He looked across at Ramon. 'You tell me! Why is she here?'

Rachel cast a compelling glance in Ramon's direction, and although he opened his mouth to reply he closed it again, and merely shook his head.

André's expression grew cynical. 'Ah, I see. Already you have bewitched poor Ramon again. What did you promise him if he let you in here?'

Rachel struggled to free herself. 'You are a brute!' she exclaimed fiercely.

'Why? Because I jump to obvious conclusions?'

'They're only obvious to you.'

'Oh no. Not only to me.' He released her abruptly, and she stood before him rubbing her wrist into which the blood flowed with painful intensity. 'However, it seems apparent that this is neither the time nor the place to indulge in arguments of this kind.' He rubbed the back of his hand down his cheek where the marks of her fingers could still be seen. 'Ramon. Where is she staying?'

Ramon shrugged. 'I don't know. In all honesty, André, I don't know.'

André looked at Rachel's mutinous expression and then raised his dark eyebrows thoughtfully. 'And of course you will not tell us,' he remarked bleakly.

Rachel took a deep breath. 'Why not? I've got nothing to hide. Besides, I know you well enough to realise that if I refuse to tell you you have only to make half a dozen phone calls to find out.' She smoothed her hair behind her ears. 'I'm staying at the Empress Hotel. It's in one of those small streets behind Bay Street.'

André's eyes darkened. 'I know it. It's little more than a *pension*! And it has a doubtful reputation. Why in hell are you staying there? Why aren't you at one of the decent hotels, or a beach club? As my wife, you would be entitled——'

Rachel glared at him. 'But I'm not here as your wife! My name is Jardin—*Miss* Jardin!'

André's expression was grim. 'Nevertheless, you are still my wife, Rachel, and until you are not——'

'Don't you threaten me, André!' she exclaimed furiously. 'What I do is my affair, and mine only. Or do you want to make it otherwise, with your—your—*girlfriend* looking on!' Her deliberate attempt to antagonise him succeeded, and she stepped back from the burning anger in his eyes.

Controlling himself, he turned to Ramon. 'We have

to go, Ramon. Leonie's parents are expecting us. I wanted to discuss the new extension, but that can wait until tomorrow.'

'Yes, André,' Ramon nodded.

'That's all, then.' André took Leonie's elbow in his fingers. Then he glanced back at Rachel. 'Oh, and Ramon! See that—my wife—gets back to her hotel, will you?'

'Of course.' Ramon nodded again.

'Good.' André turned to go, and Rachel turned away, willing him to go quickly. She couldn't maintain this mask of indifference much longer, but she refused to make a fool of herself in front of him or his proposed fiancée. Ramon walked with them to the outer door, and she heard the rumble of male voices as André's bodyguard joined them. He went nowhere without an escort, and Rachel felt that chilling feeling envelop her again. The doors closed, and Ramon came back into the room, closing the inner door behind him. Then and only then did Rachel's composure desert her, and she sank down weakly on to the chair she had previously occupied and buried her face in her hands.

Ramon came to her side, sinking down on to his knees beside her chair and forcing her fingers away from tear-wet eyes. 'Hey,' he said softly, 'what is all this?'

Rachel brushed the tears away with a hasty finger. 'Nothing,' she denied miserably. 'It was just—well—*everything!*'

Ramon frowned. 'You could hardly expect André to feel kindly disposed towards you,' he said reasonably. 'Naturally he was cruel. You were pretty cruel to him yourself.'

'I know, I know. Oh, Ramon, my journey here——'
She lifted her shoulders hopelessly. 'It's all been for
nothing. I couldn't ask him for anything now.'

'And what did you come to ask him?'

She shook her head. 'I'd rather not discuss it,' she
said quietly.

Ramon gave her a regretful smile, and rose to his
feet. 'So what will you do now?'

'Go back to England,' she replied, rising too.

Ramon studied her green eyes which still glinted
with unshed tears. 'Tell me something,' he said softly.
'Was it money?'

Rachel coloured. 'I'd like to leave now,' she said,
evading a reply. 'I—I can easily get a cab. Th-thank
you, Ramon, for everything.'

Ramon shook his head. 'You'll get no cabs here,' he
remarked sardonically. 'This isn't the West End of
London, you know. Come, my car is outside. I will take
you back to your hotel. After all, that is what André
instructed me to do.'

Rachel hadn't the heart to refuse. Instead, she
accepted his offer passively, and after he had made the
necessary arrangements with his manager, she accompanied him out of the side door on to the car-park.
They were immediately joined by a tall, broad man
who looked rather like a wrestler in city clothes, and
Rachel glanced at Ramon in wonder.

'You, too,' she murmured incredulously.

Ramon shrugged defensively. 'You can't be too careful at night,' he remarked smoothly. 'Henry doesn't
intrude. But when he's around, nor does anyone else!'

Rachel glanced again at the huge black man who
walked just behind them. 'But why?' she exclaimed.

'Why?'

Ramon halted beside a low-slung white limousine, and inserted his key in the lock. Swinging open the passenger door, he helped Rachel inside. Then he walked round and slid in beside her, behind the wheel. Henry climbed into the back, levering his bulk on to the softly padded seats almost silently. Rachel looked at Ramon, waiting for his answer, and with a gesture he said:

'As the owner of the casino at Pointe St. Auguste, I have many enemies.' He swung the limousine round in an arc and allowed it to run smoothly down the ramp on to the road. 'All my clients can't be winners!'

'But that's ridiculous!' gasped Rachel, staring at him. 'Oh, Ramon, I thought you were free of this cage that surrounds the Sanchez family, but you're not— you're not!'

Ramon glanced her way. 'Don't we all have cages, of one kind or another?' he queried gently. 'Do you think you are freer now, living the life you have chosen?'

Rachel did not immediately reply, but looked out on the beauty of the night. She could inhale a thousand perfumes at a breath of the many flowering shrubs and trees, and in the car's headlights the brilliance of poinciana and hibiscus, growing in profusion by the roadside, excited the senses. There was a magic about the place, she had to admit, and in honesty the thought of returning to London wrapped in the drabness of January was not appealing. But freedom was a mental as well as a physical thing, and while money could buy many things, it could not buy happiness, this she had discovered. For money had seemed to create all the problems in her life.

Now she said: 'No one is ever completely free. But freedom comprises many things, and bars need not be tangible things. Some people make bars where no bars exist.'

Ramon sighed. 'I guess you're talking about André.'

'I guess I am.'

'He only wanted what was best for you.'

'You think so?' Rachel's voice was impassioned suddenly. 'He took me—he moulded me—he controlled me! All he wanted was a puppet on a string!'

'He made you unhappy?'

'Yes! *Yes!*' Rachel was adamant.

'But you loved him.' He frowned. 'At least—so you said.'

'I did!' Rachel bit her lip until she tasted blood in her mouth. 'Of course I loved him. But then I discovered that the man I loved bore no resemblance to the man I married!'

'You're talking in riddles.' Ramon sounded impatient.

'No, I'm not. Once we were married—once André took me to Conchera, I was expected to fall in with his every wish!' She gave a deep sigh. 'I wasn't even allowed to go out alone!'

'You were André Sanchez's wife. You were vulnerable,' intoned Ramon, and Rachel thought he sounded a little like André used to sound.

'How was I vulnerable?' she snapped. 'No one troubled me! No one knew me! Why couldn't I act like any other tourist in Nassau?'

Ramon swung the wheel through his fingers. 'We are at *impasse*,' he commented, controlling any annoyance he might have felt at her avowals of injustice. 'You cannot see my way—André's way—and I cannot see yours.'

'You used to be able to.'

'I was much younger then. I think I have matured now, Rachel!'

'And I have not?' she asked chokingly.

'Maybe so,' he agreed quietly, and Rachel turned and stared out of the car's windows. Thereafter they did not speak, and not until they reached her hotel did Ramon break the uneasy silence which had fallen.

Then he said: 'You know, Rachel, that I would do anything to make you smile again. My feelings for you were always transparent. They have not changed.'

The car was still and he turned towards her, his arm along the back of the seat. He seemed totally unaware of his man in the back seat, but Rachel was not, and she could not relax as she would have done had they been alone. Instead, she said: 'You're very kind, Ramon. If it is any consolation, you've made me feel a little better.'

Ramon touched the softness of her hair with a lazy hand. 'You're a very beautiful woman, Rachel,' he murmured, 'as I said before. If André does divorce you, will you marry again?'

Rachel bent her head. 'That's a little difficult to say,' she prevaricated.

Ramon straightened, and swung round in his seat. 'Yes, it is,' he agreed. 'I'm sorry. Goodnight, Rachel.'

'Goodnight, Ramon.'

Rachel slid out of the car, appreciating its length and luxury. It had attracted quite a crowd of sightseers in a street like this, and she hastened inside before anyone should attempt to prevent her. She heard the limousine glide away, and her shoulders sagged. Was that all there was to be? Was that what she had come here for? Was her defeat so complete? She shook her head wearily, and climbed the stairs to her room. Outside, the town of Nassau was still alive and full of noise and excitement, but in her room, that small cubicle whose only claim to air-conditioning was provided by the slowly revolving fan in the ceiling, she sought the bleakness of her lonely bed and a sleeping tablet to dispel the memories that persisted in haunting her tired brain. Tonight, even the narcotic powers of the drug gave her no relief from the tortuous train of her thoughts, and she lay on her back staring at the night sky through the casement wondering whether there was some point in her life where everything started to go so wrong.

She considered her father, back home in London, waiting for news from her that his immediate problems were over. Was he managing adequately without her? Was he eating? And more importantly, had he found that bottle she had hidden so carefully in the bath-room cabinet?

She rolled on to her stomach, refusing to give way yet again to the self-pitying tears that threatened continually. Feeling sorry for herself would solve nothing and would merely make her eyes conspicuously puffy in the morning. The management of this small hotel were curious enough about her as it was without providing them with further room for gossip. Not that it mattered now, of course. This was probably her last night in Nassau.

The sky was ablaze with stars, and somewhere on New Providence or one of the outlying islands André

Sanchez was sleeping. Was she in his thoughts as he was in hers? She doubted it very much. She was alone, but the chances that he was alone also were extremely limited. That woman, Leonie, she was not the type to withhold her favours, and André was a man with strong, passionate emotions, Rachel knew that so well from experience. And why was it that after all that had happened, all the hateful things he had done, all she could remember was the lean strength of his body and the demanding pressure of his mouth?

CHAPTER TWO

DESPITE her disturbed state of mind Rachel eventually slept, to be awoken by the sound of someone knocking rather vigorously at her door. At first it was difficult to remember where she was, the sleeping tablet still confusing her brain, but as she roused herself everything came flooding back to her with depressing clarity. Blinking, she stared at the travelling clock on her bedside table and saw that it was barely nine o'clock. Who on earth could be waking her at this hour?

Calling: 'Wait a minute!' she crawled out of bed, groping for the cream silk dressing-gown she had left lying on the footboard and pulling it on, she tied the belt tightly about her slim waist. Smoothing back her tousled hair, she opened the door and stared rather incomprehensively at the young man who stood on the threshold. Frowning, she realised she knew him. It was André's youngest brother Vittorio.

Stepping back, she said blankly: 'What do you want?'

Vittorio smiled. When last she had seen him he had been a schoolboy of sixteen or thereabouts. Now he was an adult, and attractive as all the Sanchez brothers were attractive. 'What a greeting!' he complained indignantly. 'Aren't you pleased to see me?'

Rachel sighed. She was in no mood to be polite. 'Not particularly,' she replied. 'Why are you here?'

Vittorio stepped past her into the room, looking about him with critical eyes. 'What a dump!' he pronounced, wrinkling his nose.

Rachel clenched her fists. 'I don't recall asking your opinion,' she bit out angrily. 'Now will you please state your business or leave?'

Vittorio lifted her suitcase on to the bed, and flicked it open. 'Pack your things,' he advised pleasantly. 'We're leaving!'

Rachel stared at him in astonishment at first, and then with something approaching frustration. 'Just who do you think you are, coming here, giving me orders?' she exclaimed. 'I am certainly going to pack— but in my own good time, and then I shall be leaving— for the airport!'

Vittorio shook his head. 'I think not, Rachel.'

'What do you mean, you think not? I'm free, white, and over twenty-one. I can do what I like.'

'No, you can't, at least not here,' he amended. 'Brother André wants to see you, and he wants you out of this hotel right now.' He half smiled. 'He'd have had you out last night, if it wouldn't have caused such a furore!'

Rachel was surprised to find she was trembling. 'I

spoke to your brother last night, and his words to me didn't involve my seeing him again. I don't believe André sent you. I think Ramon's behind this.'

Vittorio shrugged. 'I can't alter your opinion, of course, but André sent me here, believe me!'

Rachel shivered. 'Why? Why does he want to see me all of a sudden? Last night I got the impression that he wouldn't care if he didn't see me ever again.'

'Maybe he still feels the same,' observed Vittorio chillingly. 'But he has agreed to see you, so come!'

'Oh, go jump in a lake!' retorted Rachel cuttingly. 'I've no intention of humbling myself to your brother!' But even as she said the words she wanted to withdraw them. She wasn't here for her own amusement, she was here in an effort to help her father. She must not adopt this attitude, this stubbornness, this pride. If it was necessary to humble herself to André, then she must do it.

But as it happened, she was given a second chance without the need for apologies. Vittorio, standing straight and tall, delivered his ultimatum.

'André told me to tell you that if you refused to accompany me he would see to it that you were brought forcibly to him if necessary. Rachel, André is a powerful man. Don't doubt his sincerity in this.'

Rachel didn't. On New Providence the Sanchez name was synonymous with affluence and authority. Biting her lips to stop them from trembling too, she said: 'You'll have to leave for a while. I need a shower and time to pack.'

Vittorio nodded politely. 'All right. I'll come back in half an hour. Be ready!'

He strode out of the door, closing it decisively behind him, and Rachel stared at the cream panels long after the sound of his footsteps had died away. What did André want with her now? What possible reason could he have for issuing this summons? So far as he was concerned she had come here in an attempt to prevent his plans for arranging the divorce. Why, then, was he removing her from the hotel? What did he intend to do with her? After all, it was as Vittorio had said, André was a powerful man on New Providence, and by coming here she had placed herself within his sphere, within his dominance. Then she remembered Leonie again, and reason took a sane hold on her rioting thoughts. Whatever he wanted, it would not be easy for her.

In the shower, allowing the cool water to cascade over her hot skin, a multitude of possibilities plagued her. Whatever happened, she should take this opportunity that had been offered to her, and somehow make André believe that her reasons for coming to Nassau were innocent of mischief-making.

She dressed with care, choosing a flared-skirted dress in a delicious shade of tangerine. The low neckline drew attention to the smooth curve of her throat and the nape of her neck, and a matching bandeau secured her hair in place. Then she packed the few things she had brought with her and fastened her suitcase. She had barely finished adding a clear lipstick to her lips and some mascara to her thick lashes when Vittorio knocked again at her door, and she called 'Come in' as she lifted her handbag. Vittorio re-entered the room, accompanied by another man whom she assumed was his manservant, for this man took charge of her suitcase and waited until Vittorio had escorted her out of the room before closing the door and following them.

Downstairs, Rachel glanced longingly towards the restaurant. Although she wasn't hungry, she would have appreciated a cup of coffee, but as though defining her thoughts Vittorio said: 'Your bill has been taken care of, and a meal is awaiting you.'

Rachel opened her mouth to protest, and then closed it again. She might as well accept that for the time being she was under the protection of the Sanchez clan, and as such she must accept their dictates. So she allowed Vittorio to escort her through the lobby, aware of the speculative gazes of the manager and his staff who all seemed to have gathered to watch her go. She felt rather like one of those political prisoners being ushered out of the sight of the press, except that she was no politician or she would have handled this situation more delicately than she had done this far.

Outside, parked in the narrow street, another of the luxury automobiles awaited them, a convertible this time in a delicious shade of ice blue. Vittorio seated her in the back, and then got into the seat beside the driver, while the man who had carried her suitcase stowed it in the boot before joining her, bestowing a slight smile in her direction. He was a man in his fifties, and Rachel wondered whether he was aware of her identity.

In the morning light, Nassau was brilliant and colourful. Even the side streets were attractive with pastel-washed walls and pitched roofs. Children stared at them unashamedly, and groups of coloured people on street corners gossiped in the sunshine. Out of the side-streets they emerged into Rawson Square, with its straw market and piazza of shops, and beyond, the bustle of Bay Street. But the automobile turned off the square and they drove along the quay where the out-island boats were being unloaded. Rachel saw the tanks of live turtles and the piles of fresh fruit, and smelt the overpowering aroma of rum, the island's favourite beverage. There was plenty of activity at this hour of the morning, and for a few minutes her interest in her surroundings made her forget her reasons for being here, and she began to wonder where Vittorio was taking her.

Just as she was about to ask, however, the huge car drew to a halt beside a wharf where a sleek ocean-going launch was moored. Vittorio vaulted out of his seat on to the quayside and opening Rachel's door helped her out too before either of his henchmen could bestir themselves. Cupping her elbow in his hand, he said:

'Well? Beautiful, isn't she?'

Rachel looked at the launch. 'Yes—beautiful,' she echoed, rather doubtfully. She glanced at her brother-in-law. 'Where are you taking me? I thought you said André wanted to see me.'

Vittorio smiled and shrugged. 'He does, he does.' He glanced round at the two men. 'Are you ready?' and at their nod he guided her to the gangplank that led on to the vessel, but here Rachel halted firmly.

'I have a right to know where you're taking me,' she averred stubbornly. 'How do I know you're really here on André's behalf?'

Vittorio spread his hands. 'You don't, of course. Nevertheless, I can assure you we are. Now won't you go aboard? I'm taking you to Palmerina!'

'Palmerina?' Rachel frowned. 'What is Palmerina?'

Vittorio looked impatient. 'My brother's island. Now,

33

will you go aboard?'

Rachel sighed, but did not demur further. There seemed no point, and besides, he had told her her destination. What more did she need?

There was another of the menservants aboard the launch which was equipped with the usual lavish accoutrements considered commonplace by the Sanchez family. A cabin was luxuriously furnished with soft banquettes that edged the panelled walls. There was a refrigerated cabinet for drinks, hi-fi equipment, and a portable Japanese television set. In a tiny alcove beyond she could see cooking equipment, and toilet facilities. The launch was powered by a motor that could achieve racing speeds, and in the stern was a pile of skin-diving equipment. It was the kind of luxury vessel one saw advertised in magazines, and Rachel thought it rather larger than life in many respects.

Presently, when she had refused to sit in the cabin and had taken a seat on deck, the engine was started, and they moved away from the busy quayside. As the perspective of the wharf grew smaller she saw the larger vessels that used the Crown Dock, and thought that nowhere were the colours more brilliant or clearly defined than here. A vista of sea and sky, blue upon blue, blended with the white sails of ships and the luxuriance of the foliage. A faint breeze fanned her cheeks, and she slid sunglasses on to her nose to save her eyes from the glare of the sun. Reflected in the water it was a dazzling sight, and in spite of her apprehension she could not suppress the surge of euphoria that enveloped her. She looked down into the blueness of the water, wondering what it would be like to swim in its warmth again. André had taught her to water-ski

34

and to skin-dive, and when he had been at home she had been content. But when he had gone away and left her on Conchera she had desired nothing so much as escape. She had felt like a prisoner, treated now and then to the company of the gods. That wasn't what marriage was all about. She had wanted to share his life, not just be a small part of it, a part that had to be protected from the rest of the world. But André had been so adamant, and she had been so stubborn. . . .

Vittorio came to sit beside her, studying her thoughtfully. 'What are you thinking?' he queried gently. 'You are so solemn.'

Rachel sighed. 'Is it far? Palmerina, I mean.'

'No, not too far. It will take perhaps an hour. Are you so impatient?'

Rachel grimaced. 'You could say that. Do you know why he wants to see me?'

'No. I merely received my instructions like everyone else.'

'So André is still the dictator.'

'He dictates the family, yes. But that is how it should be. He is the head of the family, after all.'

'I know.' Rachel bent her head. 'Do you have a cigarette?' When they were both smoking, she asked: 'And your mother? How is she?'

'My mother is very well, thank you.'

'And does she live on Palmerina too?'

Vittorio blew a smoke ring. 'No. She lives with me and Irena on Veros, an island some short distance from Palmerina.'

Rachel frowned running mentally through the remaining members of André's family. He had three brothers and two sisters. Marcus was thirty-four, and the second eldest son. 'What about Lilaine and Marcus?' she queried automatically.

'Marcus is married and lives in Rio de Janeiro,' replied Vittorio dispassionately. 'Lilaine is dead!'

'Dead!' Rachel was horrified. 'But how?'

Vittorio studied the tip of his cigarette. 'She was kidnapped on a trip to the States.'

'Kidnapped! Oh no! But ...' Rachel halted uncertainly.

Vittorio's dark eyes flickered over her. 'You're wondering whether a ransom was demanded and whether we paid it, aren't you?' Rachel bent her head and he went on: 'The answer in both cases is yes. But the police were involved, and at the end they killed her!'

Rachel shook her head disbelievingly. 'But she was so young! How terrible!' It was unbelievable. 'Did—did they get the men?'

'Oh yes.' Vittorio sounded very certain. 'André dealt with everything.' And the way he said everything had a final ring to it as though André could be relied upon to do what was best for all concerned. But the news of Lilaine's death had been a shock, and Rachel felt a fleeting anxiety, almost as though in some way Vittorio had revealed the vulnerability André had always been so conscious of; so overly conscious, Rachel had always thought. Shrugging these disquieting thoughts away, she tried to continue taking an interest in the islands they were passing, small atolls with little more than rock and sand to commend them, but a little of the brilliance had gone out of the day.

Vittorio disappeared down to the cabin soon afterwards and when he returned he was carrying a tray on which reposed a gleaming coffee pot, warm rolls and curls of butter, and an apricot conserve. Rachel looked up into Vittorio's face in amazement.

'But how marvellous!' she exclaimed. 'Did you do this?'

Vittorio smiled. 'I helped,' he commented lazily. Settling himself comfortably beside her, he went on: 'Now, you talk to me. Tell me about yourself. What have you been doing these past five years?'

Rachel flushed. 'Just living, I suppose. Helping Father in the store, keeping house....'

Buttering a roll she took a bite of the crisp crust, and Vittorio looked amused at her enjoyment. 'Tell me,' he said, suddenly, 'didn't you ever regret leaving? Didn't you miss—well—all this?'

Rachel lifted her shoulders eloquently. 'To begin with, when I was still young and foolish.'

Vittorio uttered an exclamation. 'You are still young. What age are you now? Twenty-two—twenty-three?'

'I'm twenty-five, and you know it,' she retorted, with a smile. 'How about you? Are you finished your schooling?'

Vittorio looked indignant. 'Of course,' he retorted, impatiently. 'I am almost twenty-two myself now. I spent two years at college in the States, but at last I am home for good.'

'To do what?'

He shrugged. 'Who knows? I am in André's employ until he decides I am old enough to act on my own initiative, as Ramon is now.'

Rachel shook her head. The code of ethics practised by the Sanchez family had always intrigued her. There was never any family dispute. André was the head of the family, and therefore André made the decisions.

And that was what she could not accept. They were all prepared to subjugate their desires to the good of the whole, and she had to admit, if she was honest, it worked admirably.

Later Vittorio offered her a cigarette and they smoked companionably discussing less personal topics. Vittorio seemed to sense that she did not wish to discuss her reasons for being in the Bahamas, and she refrained from questioning him too closely about his plans. Eventually, when she was beginning to wonder how much further they would have to go, Vittorio got to his feet, and leaning on the rail indicated an island with his hand.

'See!' he said, pointing. 'Palmerina!'

Rising out of the azure waters was a small island, lushly foliaged, palms fringing the coral sands, reaching almost to the shoreline in places. From the launch the island appeared deserted, the hinterland rising to shallow hills, overgrown with a forest of trees. To Rachel, expecting the civilised cultivation she had experienced on Conchera, Palmerina was wild and primitive and much more beautiful.

'Well?' said Vittorio, glancing her way as the launch negotiated the perils of the reef. 'What do you think?' He smiled. 'It's not what you expected, is it?'

'Frankly, no. Where is André's house?'

'Inland. There's a lagoon, you'll see.'

The launch drifted in with the tide, and now Rachel could see a wooden jetty which projected some feet into the water. The launch bumped gently against its sides, and was moored by one of the men before Vittorio leapt out on to the wooden boards. He put a hand down to Rachel and she climbed out too, swaying a little after the rhythm of the boat.

Then she looked about her. Away in both directions the beach curved out of sight while the foliage she had seen from the launch was just as dense close at hand but interspersed with tropical blossoms of hibiscus and oleander. Ahead, a narrow road ran from the jetty into the trees and parked on this narrow road was a small utility vehicle with a driver behind the wheel. Collecting her case, Vittorio escorted her to the vehicle, smiling a greeting to the black-skinned boy who climbed out to offer Vittorio the seat behind the wheel. Rachel was seated beside him and the boy climbed in the back. Then, leaving the two men behind them, they drove away.

The track wound between the trees for some distance and then they gathered speed up an incline emerging through a belt of pines whose scent was sweet and crisp on to a ridge. They were crossing to the other side of the island and as they began the downward sweep Rachel saw the lagoon nestling on the valley floor. Now she could see a cluster of roofs that indicated that there was a village, and beyond, standing square to the lagoon was André's house, its roof contrasting with the others because it had red tiles. The lagoon had a channel at the furthest side which led to the sea, and Rachel commented on this to Vittorio.

'It is possible to sail round the island and reach the house through the channel by crossing the lagoon,' he said, 'but this way is quicker, and while I should like to show you the island, I have very explicit orders.'

A quiver ran along Rachel's spine at his words. For a while she had been engrossed in her surroundings to the exclusion of everything else, but now his statement brought it all back to her, most particularly her reasons for being here. Feeling she had to say something, she said: 'It's very beautiful. More beautiful than Conchera.'

'And much less accessible,' remarked Vittorio dryly. 'Here, one can only breach the reef at one point, the one we used. André employs a guard who lives, with his dogs, in a house hidden by the trees you saw when we arrived. There is a telephone link with the house. No one reaches Palmerina without André being warned.'

'And by air?' questioned Rachel, intrigued in spite of herself.

'Impossible, except by a chopper. André uses one, of course. But the airfield is small, and so long as his is in occupation, there's little chance of anyone taking him unawares.'

'A veritable stronghold, in fact,' murmured Rachel, almost to herself.

'Yes, I suppose you could say that.' Vittorio had overheard her. 'Rachel! Don't go on with this antagonism. André's much harder now than he was. You made him so!'

'I?'

'Yes, you.' Vittorio put the vehicle into a lower gear to negotiate the curve into the village. 'André loved you, Rachel, and you destroyed that love.'

Rachel's cheeks turned scarlet. 'Everyone seems to know my husband better than I do,' she exclaimed, turning to attack rather than defence. 'André only wanted another possession, a human one this time!'

Vittorio gave her a quelling glance. 'You don't believe that!' he stated calmly, 'so don't expect me to.'

Rachel heaved a sigh. 'Well, anyway, that's all in the past. He has—Leonie, now. Who is she, by the way?'

'Leonie?' Vittorio looked thoughtful. 'Her father owns a big oil concession in Trinidad. Her name is Leonie Gardner, and her parents are of French-Canadian descent, I believe. At any rate, they're very well established in New Providence. They have a house near Nassau.'

'I see.' Rachel listened with interest. 'I—I wonder why André waited until now to get the divorce. If he has been thinking of getting married for some time, I'm surprised everything wasn't taken care of before this.' She couldn't prevent the hint of sarcasm that crept into her voice. 'After all, he arranges everything so clinically, doesn't he?' She bit her lip.

Vittorio sounded annoyed. 'He hasn't been thinking of getting married for some time,' he returned shortly. 'I must admit, I'd be chary of the institution after——' He broke off. 'Besides, André doesn't have to marry a woman before ...' He halted again. 'Goddammit, you know what I mean!'

Rachel bent her head. 'And have there been many? Women, I mean?'

Vittorio raised a lazy hand in greeting to some of the villagers that were standing by the roadside watching their progress, and then sighed. 'For someone who professes to despise my brother, you're inordinately interested in his affairs,' he observed mockingly, and Rachel's fingers gripped her bag tightly.

The vehicle was running along beside the lake now and Rachel could see a yacht anchored out in the centre. That must be André's boat. He was a keen

41

sailor and when he was home they had had some wonderful trips together. She felt a tightness in her throat and a conviction that whatever her reasons she ought not to have come here, not to the Bahamas, not to New Providence, and most definitely not to Palmerina.

As they neared the house she could see it was two-storied, with green shutters at the windows and washed in a cream paint. It was surrounded by gardens, colourful with the many varied blossoms to be found in the islands, and stood in the shade of tall, feathery palms. Double doors stood wide, opening on to a panelled hall which Rachel could see as Vittorio brought their transport to a halt at the foot of shallow steps leading on to a low veranda. Tubs of tropical plants tumbled near the entrance, while the slats of the veranda were overhung with bougainvillea. There was so much beauty and colour it almost hurt her eyes, but she removed her dark glasses and stepped out on to the paved courtyard.

Immediately, a dark-skinned woman in a scarlet dress and sparkling white apron appeared at the double doors, and stood staring at them incredulously. Rachel looked at the elderly woman, then at Vittorio.

'Why, it's Pandora!' she exclaimed, in welcome astonishment.

Vittorio nodded, and even as he did so, Pandora uttered an exclamation of delight and hastened down the veranda steps to greet her.

'Miss Rachel, Miss Rachel!' she was saying over and over again. 'You've come back!'

Rachel felt herself engulfed in a bear-like embrace and drawing back a little, she said gently: 'Oh, Pandora, it's wonderful to see you, too. Everything's changed—everything except you!'

'Oh, Mr. André! He hasn't changed,' answered Pandora, her eyes a trifle moist. 'My—my—he'll be so pleased to see you back, Miss Rachel!'

Rachel felt slightly emotional herself at this welcome, but she tried to sound casual as she said: 'I've not come to stay, Pandora. Just—just visiting, that's all.'

Pandora's face changed. 'You're not staying?' she said, aghast. 'Why are you here, then?'

Rachel sighed. 'It's a long story, Pandora. I'll tell you some other time.'

Vittorio joined them looking thoughtfully at his sisters-in-law. Then he looked at Pandora. 'Where is my brother?'

Pandora gestured with her hands. 'Out back. He's down at the boats. Shall I tell him you're here?'

Vittorio shook his head. 'No, don't bother. We'll go down. Come on, Rachel. We'll go through the house. It's quicker.'

Rachel accompanied him up the steps and through the double doorway into a marble-tiled hall. Arched doorways opened to left and right into lounges and dining areas. Some doors were closed, but those that were open revealed magnificently appointed apartments with crystal chandeliers reflected in polished wood, and soft leather furnishings. Some floors were carpeted, but others were polished and strewn with rugs and smelt deliciously of beeswax. Crossing the hall, Vittorio led the way out through another archway on to a patio tiled in a multi-patterned mosaic of muted colours. Rachel halted for a moment here. The view was magnificent, a backcloth of lake and hillside, and away to the right the channel that opened out into the ocean. The patio was broad, and beyond steps led down through lawns and flower gardens to where a pine-logged boathouse had been built beside a small wooden jetty. And it was here they found André Sanchez, working on the engine of one of his motor-boats, dressed casually in dark shorts and a dark shirt, unbuttoned to his waist. Nearby another man was working inside the boathouse, and he came out at their approach, obviously to see who was joining them. He nodded when he saw Vittorio, and André looked up, wiping his oily hands on a rag.

Rachel felt suddenly a mass of nerves, and she hovered uncertainly on the path, unwilling to venture on to the jetty. André said something to his companion, and then vaulted up the slope to their side, raking back his dark hair with a lazy hand.

'So. You came,' he remarked, unnecessarily.

Rachel bit her lip. 'I didn't have much choice.'

André half smiled. 'No, you did not, did you? Okay, Vittorio, I can take it from here. I want you to go back to Nassau and see Kingston.'

'All right.' Vittorio nodded. 'What about Ramon?'

'I'll see Ramon later,' replied André, looking thoughtful. 'You know what to do?'

'Sure.'

'Good.' André nodded, and Vittorio gave Rachel a rather amused smile, and walked away through the rose gardens and round the side of the house. Alone with André, Rachel was bereft of speech, and when he indicated that she should precede him into the house she did so with some misgivings.

Once inside, André led the way into a cool lounge

44

that overlooked the rear of the building, with the lake and the trees beyond. Excusing himself for a moment, he left her alone, and she seated herself in a soft red leather armchair by the french doors and lit a cigarette. She might as well compose herself. Until he chose to tell her why he had brought her here there was little she could do.

When he returned, he had washed his hands, and he walked over to a bell and pressed it before sitting down in the chair opposite her. When a manservant appeared a few moments later, he ordered coffee for two, and then reached for a cigar from a box on a nearby table. As he did so, Rachel studied him surreptitiously. The previous evening she had been too disturbed to register every detail about him, but now she found she enjoyed just looking at him. His limbs were tanned a deep brown and looked much more attractive than the pale bodies of men she had seen sunbathing in England. But then he lived in an ideal climate, and had that kind of colouring that took to hot weather. Besides, he had Spanish blood in his veins only slightly diluted by his English mother. His chest was darkened still further by the hairs that grew there, and she could see a silver medallion shining in the darkness. He had made no concessions to formality and Rachel wondered if it was an attempt on his part to disconcert her. He must have known she would be expecting a business-like encounter.

Getting to her feet, she moved restlessly over to an exquisitely carved relief in ebony. It was the head of an Indian, and the planes and angles of his face were almost lifelike.

'This is attractive,' she said awkwardly. 'Where did

were designed to hurt me, were they not?'

Rachel bent her head. 'How does a puppet hurt its master?'

André uttered an exclamation and stepped towards her ominously, her quiet words arousing him as no amount of anger could have done, but the manservant chose that moment to return with the tray of coffee, and Rachel returned to her seat. The man placed the tray on the low table beside her and she was forced to take charge of it, handling the silver coffee jug with trembling fingers.

'Cream and sugar?' she asked automatically as the man withdrew, but André shook his head.

'I'll take it black,' he answered abruptly, and she poured some into one of the tall pottery beakers and handed it to him, avoiding his eyes as she did so. Then she poured her own, adding cream and sugar, and sipped it rather desperately, almost as though she hoped it would provide her with strength to remain composed throughout this interview.

André did not sit, but stood by the french doors, staring out across the lake. Rachel glanced his way, registering that the rich gold curtains that blended so well with the cream tapestry-covered walls acted as a foil to the almost swarthy cast of his features. In profile she could see the strength in his face, the firm line of his chin, the angles of his cheek and jawline. She could even see the length and thickness of his lashes which had always been the only feminine thing about him.

When Rachel felt that her nerves were stretched to breaking point, he turned back to her again, and she realised he had again got himself in control. Replacing his empty beaker on the tray, he re-lit his cigar and drew on it deeply. Then he came to stand before her, looking down at her thoughtfully.

Rachel quivered, and put down her coffee rather untidily, spilling some on the tray. Fumbling for cigarettes, she was forestalled as he offered her a box from a nearby cabinet, and then when she had accepted one, lit it for her.

'Now,' he said, as she smoked vigorously, 'why are you so nervous?'

Rachel tapped ash unnecessarily into the ashtray. 'Considering you're doing everything to make me feel so, I don't see any point in that question,' she retorted, rather unevenly.

'*I* make you nervous?'

'Of course. Oh, stop fencing with me, André. Tell me why you've brought me here, and be done with it.'

André seated himself in the chair opposite her, sitting forward, legs apart, his arms resting casually on his knees. 'You came to Nassau to find me,' and as she would have argued, he continued: 'Don't bother to deny it. Ramon told me. He also told me that he believed you had not received any communication before you left, and that your reasons for being here were more personal ones, personal to you that is.'

Rachel bent her head. 'He had no right to tell you anything.'

'Why? What was your intention? To fly right back again without even telling me why you came?'

'Yes, if you must know!'

André shook his head. 'Still the same arrogance!' he muttered softly. 'So proud—so unwilling to *ask* for anything!'

'I came to see you,' Rachel flared indignantly. 'I was

willing to ask all right. I agreed to humble myself before the mighty André Sanchez! But even I have feelings!'

'And I do not?' André's voice was taut. 'Rachel, you are the most exasperating and infuriating woman I have ever met! Here you have a chance, a real opportunity to speak reasonably with me, and what are you doing? I will tell you. You are selfishly absorbed with your own pride, your own humiliation, your own feelings!'

Rachel got unsteadily to her feet. 'What's the point in continuing this argument?'

'You intend to go back to London?' André looked up at her with narrowed eyes.

Rachel turned away, groping for the back of her chair, anything to give her support. She was a fool, a crazy fool, here was her chance, here was her opportunity as he had said, and she was too proud to take it. Maybe if she had not been aware of his desire for a divorce it would have been easier to accept his contempt, but now all she could think was that he would find it all so amusing to relate to Leonie Gardner.

She caught her breath, as she recalled her promise to her father. How could she jeopardise his future, his chance of happiness, because of foolish pride? She ran her tongue over dry lips. It was no good behaving in this manner. She stiffened her shoulders. In this, at least, André was right. She was behaving selfishly, only thinking of her own mortification. But it was terribly difficult to suppress the desire to tell him to keep his patronage for somebody else, and destroy that mask of indifferent politeness once and for all. He was so controlled, so much the master of the situation, while she was a trembling mass of nerves and sensations. She wanted to smash his disciplined restraint and arouse him to a full awareness of her again. But she quelled such feline irresponsibilities, and finally said with difficulty: 'I've considered what you've said, and perhaps I have been a little impulsive.'

André lay back in his chair studying her with a piercing scrutiny. She wondered what he was thinking, what pleasure her submission has given him. In his place she doubted whether she could have been so restrained. She would have been unable to prevent a taunting reproof. But André merely moved his shoulders in an expressive gesture, and said:

'All right, Rachel, sit down, and tell me why you came.'

Rachel subsided on to her chair again wishing he would not stare at her so intently. It was difficult to think coherently with his eyes wandering over her body, and woman that she was she wondered whether he still found her attractive. She was slimmer, of course, but things hadn't been easy one way and another, and she had never eaten a lot. But she kept her hair in good condition, and her skin was as soft and smooth as it ever was. And the tangerine dress suited her creamy colouring. But if he found anything attractive about her he did not show it and there was a chilling insensitivity about the quality of his appraisal.

It was difficult to know where to begin, so she said slowly: 'It's my father.'

André showed no surprise. 'As it ever was,' he commented dryly.

Rachel's eyes flickered, and then she sighed. 'As you say.' Her tone was forcibly subdued. 'I don't know how to tell you this.' She shook her head a trifle desperately. 'I couldn't believe it myself when I first heard it.' She sought about for words to express herself. 'It's to do with the store—or at least the antiques themselves.'

André leaned forward again. 'Go on. Has your father gotten into debt? Is the store losing money? The antique business can be a pretty precarious proposition, but your father knew that when we bought the place.'

'I know, I know.' Rachel compressed her lips. 'Oh, if it only was money,' she exclaimed passionately. 'We could have sold the store!'

'Without informing me?' queried André coldly.

Rachel sighed. 'You gave the store to Father,' she reminded him quietly.

'I know that!' muttered André grimly. 'But without his source of livelihood, what would your father do? Or you either, for that matter?'

Rachel lifted her shoulders expressively. 'When you bought the store, my mother was newly dead, and my father was rapidly becoming a self-pitying creature, drinking himself into a pleasanter world.' She sighed again. 'You gave him back his self-respect, you installed him in the store, and made him whole again.'

André shrugged. 'So what has gone wrong? Has he started drinking again?'

Rachel spread her hands. 'The business wasn't doing too well about eighteen months ago and he was approached by some men, I don't know who they were, but they offered him a kind of deal. If he agreed to sell some of their stuff for them, he would get a big commission.'

'Oh God!' André looked disgusted and got to his

feet. 'So that's it!' he muttered impatiently. 'Did you know about it?'

Rachel shook her head vigorously. 'Of course not. Do you think I'd have let him agree to something like that?' She hunched her shoulders. 'I didn't know a thing about it until three weeks ago. Then my father told me what was going on. The police had been to the store while I was out and although they hadn't accused him of anything, they'd certainly frightened him. To be brief, he refused to take anything else from these men, and now he's threatened with exposure or blackmail!'

André said nothing, but crossing to a cabinet he opened it to reveal a comprehensive display of alcohol. Taking a glass, he poured himself a stiff measure of whisky and swallowed it at a gulp. Then he lit another cigar and came back to her, looking down at her rather exasperatedly.

'So you came to me,' he stated bluntly.

'Yes.' Rachel linked and unlinked her fingers. 'I'm sorry—but there didn't seem anyone else I could turn to.'

André uttered an expletive. 'Why didn't you come to me eighteen months ago when the business first started to go downhill?'

Rachel shook her head. 'I don't know. I suppose at first I didn't think it was serious, I thought things would pick up, and after they did I never questioned where the money came from.'

'And the money I sent you?'

Rachel bit her lip hard. 'We used that, too. Father needed a car to get about—and then he did some entertaining!'

'Your father spent the money?' André's tones were violent.

'Some of it,' she prevaricated.

'Most of it,' he ground out heavily. 'And now I suppose he's resorted to the bottle again!'

Rachel shrugged. 'Sometimes,' she had to admit. 'But he tries hard—he really does! Only nothing ever seems to go right for him.'

'*He tries hard!*' mimicked André relentlessly. 'Your father is a born loser!'

'That's not his fault!'

'No, and it's not mine either!' André said savagely. 'When I met you you were trying to pick your father up after one disaster! Now you're trying to pick him up after another! And they're all his own fault! He must have known what he was running into, just as when your mother died he knew that turning to drink wouldn't do anything constructive towards his livelihood!'

Rachel had to defend her parent. 'When my mother died he lost his job, I know, but Mr. Lorrimer didn't understand how much Father felt my mother's loss!'

André looked sceptical. 'I agree, Lorrimer didn't understand, but then nor do I! It's a common failing, just as you've never understood me!'

Rachel got to her feet. 'So you're not going to help us?'

André glared at her. 'Stop jumping to conclusions! I didn't say that.'

'You implied it!' Rachel was defensive.

'Implied? Implied? What does that word mean? An implication means many things.' He raked his hand through his hair. 'You can't expect to come here and tell me that my father-in-law has been casually swindling me for the past five years and not get any reaction!'

'The money you sent me was mine.'

'I agree. But you didn't spend it, did you? And from the location of the hotel you chose here, you haven't saved it either! The *Empress* Hotel!' He almost spat out the words.

Rachel pressed a hand to her throat. 'I don't think there's anything constructive to be gathered by my staying here,' she ventured. 'I—I've got to go back to London. Apart from anything else, I can't afford to stay here any longer.'

'*Afford!* Don't use that word to me,' he said angrily. 'As for the rest, you can give up any ideas of leaving for the next few days!'

Rachel stared at him. 'And where am I supposed to stay?' She squared her shoulders. 'Your brother and his henchman cancelled my reservation at the hotel!'

André looked at her intently. 'You can stay with my mother, on Veros. It's an island not far from Palmerina.'

Rachel gasped, 'I couldn't stay with your mother!'

'Why not? She knows you're here.'

Rachel swept back her hair, looping it behind her ears. 'You must know that would be impossible,' she exclaimed. 'After all that's happened, I wouldn't expect your mother to want me there.'

'Nevertheless, that is where you will stay,' he replied adamantly.

'You can't order me now, André.'

'Can't I? In this instance, I think I can. Unless, of course, you want to stay here.' His eyes darkened suddenly, and he ran the fingers of one hand along the smooth bare skin of her forearm. 'It might be quite amusing at that. Taking a wife—as a mistress!'

Rachel's cheeks burned. 'Don't you have one of them already?' she asked insolently, taking refuge from her treacherous emotions in rudeness.

André's eyebrows ascended. 'I've never possessed such a virago as you, Rachel,' he replied distinctly, and she turned away from him, hating him for humiliating her still further.

'I—I'll stay—with your mother,' she murmured, in a small voice.

'I rather thought you might,' he said dampeningly, and she realised the whole gambit had been yet another attempt to show her exactly what he thought of her. For the first time she felt a sense of frustration with her father for forcing her into this situation. He had had no misgivings about sending her here, apparently unaware, or uncaring, that she might be humiliated by the man who had once been the whole axis on which her world turned, and who now regarded her with less esteem than one of the serving girls in his employ.

CHAPTER THREE

THE helicopter which André had piloted from Palmerina to Veros landed in a field only a short way from his mother's house, and Rachel climbed out of its bubble-like interior with quaking legs and a nervous stomach. She had no idea what kind of reception she would receive, and she could not accept that André's mother would find it easy to be civil to her after all that had happened. She thanked Gilroy, one of André's bodyguard, who assisted her to alight, and then looked back reluctantly at her husband who was extricating himself from behind the controls. Dressed formally now in a biscuit-coloured lounge suit and a cream shirt, he looked every inch the businessman he was.

He dropped down on to the grass beside her issuing instructions to the other man, Sheridan, and then looked down at her thoughtfully.

'You look scared stiff,' he remarked, rather impatiently. 'Why? I thought you liked my mother. She is a countrywoman of yours, after all.'

Rachel sighed. 'Of course I like your mother. It's just—well, you're her son!'

He shrugged and took her arm to guide her across the field towards the attractive house which could be seen in the distance. 'And you're still her daughter-in-law,' he reminded her softly.

Rachel glanced at him swiftly. 'But not for long,' she said sharply, and he inclined his head.

'You could be right,' he agreed annoyingly.

Rachel bit her lip. 'André, about Lilaine——'

His eyes were guarded. 'What about Lilaine?'

'Vittorio told me. I'm so sorry. I wanted to ask you whether I should mention it to your mother or not.'

André considered her question gravely. 'My mother has got over the worst of it now,' he said at last. 'Three years is a long time. But maybe it would be as well to let her raise the subject in her own good time.'

Rachel shook her head. 'But why did it happen? It

all seems completely crazy!'

André's eyes darkened. 'You would never accept that the improbable was not impossible, would you, Rachel?' he asked harshly.

Rachel looked away from the anger in his eyes. She knew to what he was referring, but she still found it hard to believe that such things could happen to people around her.

However, just at that moment their attention was distracted by the sight of a small girl who had darted out of the house in the distance and who was running rapidly across the grass towards them. She couldn't have been more than three or four, and was round and chubby with rosy cheeks and dark curly hair. Rachel looked at André in surprise.

'Who is that?' she cried, in astonishment. 'Oh, she's adorable!'

André ignored her, but strode ahead to swing the little girl up into his arms, where she clung lovingly round his neck, rubbing her cheek against his. Then he turned back to Rachel. 'This is Maria,' he said, his eyes expressionless. 'The daughter of my brother, Marcus, and his wife, Olivia.'

'Oh!' Rachel swallowed hard. 'Are they here?'

'No, they are holidaying in Europe. Maria is staying with her grandmother while they are away, are you not, Maria?' He smiled at the child, a complete transformation from the chilling coldness with which he had looked at his wife. 'Have you been a good girl?'

Trying not to feel hurt at André's attitude, Rachel stepped forward and smiled at the little girl. 'Hello, Maria,' she said gently. 'I'm very pleased to meet you.'

Maria studied her silently, and then turned back to

her uncle. 'Who is that?' she asked clearly.

André frowned, and stood her down on her sturdy little legs. 'This is your Aunt Rachel,' he replied, with obvious reluctance.

'My aunt?' exclaimed the little girl with surprise. 'But where is Aunt Leonie?'

Rachel's cheeks burned, but she would not let André see her embarrassment. Instead, she went down on her haunches beside the child and said: 'You will see Aunt Leonie another day. Now, will you show me where your grandmother is? I'd like to meet her, too.'

Maria glanced up at her uncle, and then back at Rachel. 'All right,' she agreed, with a nod, and let Rachel take her hand. 'Have you come to stay?'

'For a little while,' agreed Rachel. 'Do you like staying here?'

'Oh yes!' Maria frowned. 'Do you have any boys or girls for me to play with?' She sighed. 'There's only Tottie here, and she doesn't run very fast.'

Rachel bit her lip. 'I'm afraid I don't have any boys or girls at all,' she said, wondering whether André was aware of the tensions that Maria was creating. Had he known and realised what coming here and seeing Maria would do to her? If so, then it was a cruel plan indeed.

André strode ahead of them, and opened the gate that led into the garden of his mother's house, and Rachel took a moment to look about her. The house was similar to, but smaller than, André's, and as it was situated amongst palms above a coral beach, it was much more easily accessible. As they reached the doors, a young woman came out and stood watching their progress, a hand raised to shade her eyes. Rachel recognised her as her sister-in-law Irena. Irena was a little older than she was, and Rachel speculated that she must be about twenty-seven or eight now. Tall, and very thin, with angular features, she was like and yet unlike the other members of the family. Perhaps not marrying had soured her, although when Rachel had known her last she had not been so old, but there had always been that awareness about her that she was not as attractive as the other members of the Sanchez family and she had resented this terribly. She had never liked Rachel, but she had been forced to accept her, and when Rachel had at last deserted André to return to England after that last terrible quarrel, she had willingly made all the arrangements. Thinking back to that terrible day, Rachel shivered even in the heat of the noonday sun, and wondered how Irena would react seeing her here again, even if it was only a temporary arrangement.

André greeted his sister, and Irena gave Rachel a cool nod, successfully banishing any necessity to utter platitudes that would mean absolutely nothing to either of them.

'Mother is waiting lunch for you,' she said, to her brother. 'You're late.'

André shrugged impatiently. 'There were things to do,' he replied vaguely. He looked back at Rachel, still holding Maria's hand, and talking desultorily to the child. 'Come along,' he urged. 'Maria! Go and find Tottie. She's probably looking for you.'

Maria looked mutinous. 'But I want to eat with you, Uncle André,' she pleaded.

'Not today, sweetheart. Run along, there's a good girl.'

Maria heaved a sigh, but she trudged away as they entered the house, giving Rachel a faint smile. Rachel felt a tugging at her heart, but then she gave her attention to the exquisite appointments of the house. It had the same taste and distinction as the house on Palmerina, and the cool hall was redolent with the scent of flowers placed in vases everywhere. The hall opened into a long light lounge that ran from front to back of the building, and it was here they found André's mother, seated on a striped divan reading a newspaper. Madam Sanchez rose at their entrance, and Rachel saw how little she had changed. Widowed eighteen years ago, and left with six children and an empire to control, she had managed admirably, and as soon as André was old enough, he had taken the weight of the organisation from her shoulders. Her husband had been a shrewd businessman, investing his money wisely, and obtaining much of his resources from earlier explorations in South American mining. Nevertheless, André's knowledge and expertise had revitalised the organisation, and now it ran on oiled wheels, each of the sons being allotted a share of the business as soon as they were capable enough to handle it. And behind them all, Madam Sanchez exercised her own will, helping and advising whenever necessary, but never intruding. She was tall and slim and dark, like her children, and if there were several more grey hairs at her temples then it was only to be expected after all she had suffered both with her husband, and her daughter. Rachel knew the break-up of André's marriage had affected her excessively, but Rachel had found it impossible at that time to confide in her, or to seek her advice.

Now Madam Sanchez came to greet her, a faint smile

hovering about her lips. 'So, Rachel, you have come back,' she said consideringly. 'Nevertheless, I am pleased to see you!'

Rachel hovered by the entrance, unable to relax. 'Hello—madam,' she murmured awkwardly.

Madam Sanchez frowned. 'What is this? *Madam?* You used to call me Mother. Is it so impossible for you to do so again?'

Rachel coloured. 'Of course not, but—well——' She halted uncertainly.

André strolled across to the cocktail cabinet. 'I think Rachel needs a drink,' he remarked laconically. 'Something to calm her nerves!'

Rachel cast him an angry glance, but his mother merely smiled. 'Yes, perhaps you are right, André. After all, I can understand that Rachel will be nervous of us—how did she use to put it? *En masse!* Yes, that is right, *en masse!*'

André's lips twitched, and Rachel clenched her fists. 'I——I—I'm sure you would rather I stayed in a hotel in Nassau,' she began indignantly.

Madam Sanchez moved across to her, laying her hands on Rachel's shoulders. 'And I am sure that is not so,' she said quietly. 'Do not resent us so much, little one. We cannot resist the chance to mock you a little. After all, you left us—we did not make you go.'

Rachel bit her lip. 'And this was part of the reason,' she exclaimed passionately, aware of Irena, standing by the window and enjoying this scene. 'You always were a family, together. I was the outsider. I was the one who didn't understand!'

André swung round, his eyes cold and intense. 'You didn't understand, I agree,' he said bleakly. Then he

61

swallowed his drink. 'Oh, for God's sake, Mother, don't let's start all that over again, the minute she arrives!'

Madam Sanchez shrugged. 'I merely wanted Rachel to know that she is a Sanchez, and no matter what happens, she will remain a Sanchez, and as such she is entitled to our protection.'

André studied the contents of his glass intently. 'A divorce is final, Mother,' he said roughly.

Madam Sanchez lifted her shoulders, and turned to him. 'You were married in church, André, in the sight of God, and nothing can change that!'

Rachel pressed a hand to her stomach. 'Oh, please,' she began. 'I'll get out of your hair just as soon as you let me!'

André looked across at her. 'You'll go when I say so, and not before,' he replied, and turned abruptly back to the cabinet.

'Oh, don't let's get so intense!' exclaimed his mother, spreading her hands. 'Come, Rachel, sit with me and tell me what it is that has brought you to André.'

Rachel looked helplessly at her husband's uncompromising back. The last thing she wanted was to discuss her father's shortcomings in Irena's presence. As though sensing her discomfort, André poured her a glass of sherry and carrying it over to her, said: 'I'll explain later, Mother.'

Irena's eyebrows ascended. 'Why? Is it a secret or something?'

'No, but it is personal,' said André briefly, and his mother nodded and accepted his rebuke.

Rachel allowed Madam Sanchez to lead her to the divan on which she had earlier been sitting, and they sat together drinking their sherry and sharing small talk. They discussed Maria, and her parents' trip to Europe; they commented on the current fashions, and Madam Sanchez complimented her on her appearance. Meanwhile, André disappeared and Irena took up some sewing she had been working on by the window. It was a very companionable scene, thought Rachel cynically. No one would guess the real relationships that had existed between these people. It seemed that André had little to say to his sister, for he mostly ignored her, and Rachel wondered whether he was fully aware of the way in which she had assisted her sister-in-law to escape from his dominance. Not that Rachel had any illusions as to her reasons for doing such a thing. Madam Sanchez was doing her best to make her relax, but while the older woman had always been sympathetic to her daughter-in-law's problems, even she had been unable to understand her reasons for wanting to leave. Rachel doubted whether she had ever thought anything would come of it. And indeed, if Rachel had had the child that André so badly wanted, she probably never would.

Her stomach contracted with sudden pain. It was difficult from the distance of five years to wholly understand her own motives, and only André's intolerance served as a spur to her indignation. Maybe now that she was older, and possibly more mature, she was more tolerant herself. At any rate, seeing the child, Maria, had opened up a wound inside her that would take a very long time to heal again. She bit her lips hard. If only he had tried to understand that it had not been the desire to punish him that had sent her on that expedition with Ramon, but rather a need to prove her own individuality. The disastrous events which followed had destroyed her just as effectively as they had destroyed his love.

Thrusting these thoughts aside. she tried to concentrate on what André's mother was saying, but it was difficult when everything and everyone reminded her vividly of the pain she had suffered; was still suffering if she was wholly honest with herself. . . .

The room Madam Sanchez had allotted her was light and compact, with pastel-shaded walls and coverings in pinks and blues. The adjoining bathroom was pink as well, and the huge jars of bath crystals recalled her first initiation into extravagant living. It was soon after she had met André and he had taken her to the apartment he had leased in London. It had been a huge place, with luxurious appointments of a kind Rachel had never seen before. She had wandered around in a daze, fingering the cut-glass decanter and silverware, the softness of silk upholstery, the smoothness of polished rosewood, the exquisite rarity of old things that went for thousands at auctions. It had none of the garish modernity she had grown to expect, and only the bathroom had exhibited the most up-to-date in designing.

Then André had had a telephone call, and had had to go out for a while, asking her to stay in the apartment until he returned. She had agreed, but she had grown bored after a while, and wandering into the bathroom had taken a bath in the huge bath with its beaten gold taps and jars of bath crystals in a variety of shades. She had sprinkled them into the water liberally, and had soaked in the scented depths for over an hour. When she emerged, she had wrapped herself in a white bathrobe she had found on the bathroom door, and entered the lounge to get herself a cigarette when André returned unexpectedly and found her there. She remembered she had felt awfully embarrassed. For she had been only eighteen in those days while André was already a mature man of thirty-three. But his amusement at her plight had swiftly turned to passion when he touched her and Rachel had responded with all the warmth and generosity of her loving nature. Of course, she had had other boy-friends, but no one so experienced as André, and that had been the start of their affair. She had known from the start that she was playing a dangerous game getting involved with a man like André Sanchez, but she had been unable to resist him, and when his time in England drew to a close she was desperate with love for him. But she had expected nothing of him, and she had been wild with delight when he had told her he couldn't live without her and wanted to marry her. She hadn't even then really appreciated how much she really meant to him, and it took months of being with him, of sharing his days and his nights, to assure her that it was no fleeting dream. It wasn't until much later that she began to feel the constraint he was gradually putting upon her or realise that he expected her to fall in with all *his* plans. She was a *Sanchez*! How she had grown to hate that sentence which once had sent a shiver of ecstasy along her spine!

She walked to the balcony doors and thrust them open, stepping out on to the balcony and inhaling the night air. Her room overlooked the beach, and she could see the shadows lengthening quickly as darkness fell. Already the day was almost over, and she still had no idea what, if anything, André intended to do about her father. Lunch had been a constrained meal, and afterwards André and his mother had disappeared into what seemed to be a study, obviously to discuss Rachel's problems. But Rachel herself was not invited to join them, and she thrust back the resentment this aroused in her, and had gone down to the beach, unwilling to remain in the house in case Irena attempted to question her about her reasons for being there. On the beach, she had found Maria and Tottie, her coloured nanny, and had spent some time with them, making sandpies for the child and paddling with her in the shallow blue water. Later, she had returned to the house, refused the afternoon tea one of the servants pressed upon her, and went to her room to take a bath.

And now she was bathed and sweet-smelling, and wondering how formal dinners at Veros usually were. She did not even know if André would be there for the meal. The helicopter had taken off somewhere around five o'clock, but that could have been one of the men, Gilroy or Sheridan. She sighed. Veros was far removed from the small antique shop in the Kings Road, although the shop had its compensations. They were within reach of every art exhibition, every auction, every showing that took place, and Rachel, who enjoyed exploring art galleries and poring over old manuscripts, found plenty to fill her time. It had been difficult at first, after her break with André, to fit back into her father's life and to make a life for herself. She had grown accustomed in two years to the obsequious attention offered to every member of the Sanchez family wherever they went, and it was difficult to accept public transport as a substitute for chauffeur-driven limousines. And yet there had been a kind of excitement in the anonymity they offered, and it was good to feel anonymous in a crowd after always standing apart. She could understand a little now the problems of being recognised and the disadvantages that ordinary people couldn't appreciate, seeing only the glitter and not the boredom of it all.

Naturally, at first she had been still weak and listless, hardly recovered from the catastrophic depression that having a miscarriage could create, and unable to accept that her marriage, as she had known it, was over. But her father had been a pillar of strength at that time, and if his reasons for helping her had involved using some of the money she still possessed in an attempt to settle some of his own debts, she had been too tired to object. All she had wanted to do was hide away from the world until her mental and physical state were more adequate to support her. She had not noticed then that the shop was rarely cleaned or tidied, or that her father had spent more time at the racetrack than actually working, but when she recovered she took over these duties automatically, doing all that was needed herself, and learning quite a lot about the antique business besides. Antiques had never been her interest; she had worked in a library until her marriage to André. And yet it was through antiques that she had met him.

That was in the days soon after her mother's death, when her father was working for an old-established firm of art collectors called Lorrimers. Her mother had always possessed the driving force of their family, and when she died suddenly from an organic heart disease, he had been distraught. Rachel had been unable to console him and eventually he had taken to staying out of the house later and later every evening, spending his time propping up a bar somewhere until Rachel was frantic with worry. Naturally, his work had begun to suffer, and Mr. Lorrimer, not an understanding man at the best of times, had eventually dismissed him after twenty years' loyal service. That had been the last straw as far as her father was concerned, but in an attempt to show his sense of injustice and indignation he had gone back to the shop one afternoon after the pubs were closed and made a clumsy attempt to attack Matthew Lorrimer. The shop had been deserted at the time, and maybe he would have succeeded in his intention to knock the other man down had not a customer arrived at that moment and prevented him by overpowering him from behind. That man had been André Sanchez, and although Lorrimer had wanted to call the police, Sanchez had suggested that it might be more humane to simply call the man's family and have them take him home. As her father had been too befuddled to think clearly by this time, Rachel had been called, and she had gone to the shop with a sinking heart. André Sanchez was still there, and his car was outside, he had offered to run them home. She had accepted gratefully, instantly aware of the attractions of the man himself.

And so it was that the dark-skinned Spaniard had begun to take an interest in her, pursuing her with ruthless determination with the single-minded strength of purpose he applied to all his affairs, business or otherwise.

She sighed. It all seemed so long ago, another world almost, and she wondered what her reactions would

have been if André had come to her instead of the other way around. He was so detached, so self-sufficient, she could hardly believe that this was the same man who had once trembled with emotion in her arms, unable and unwilling to let her out of his sight.

At seven o'clock, she dressed in the plain black dress she had worn the previous evening for the casino, leaving her hair loose and unadorned. Apart from the gold bracelet, she had left all her jewellery on Conchera, but its simplicity suited her mood.

Downstairs, lamps illuminated the lounge and patio delicately, softening everything in their mellow glow. Madam Sanchez had not yet come down, but Irena was there, and Rachel was forced to speak to her.

'It's a beautiful night,' she commented casually.

Irena turned. In a straight sheath of green silk, she looked plain and uninteresting, a garish lipstick making her mouth a slash of colour. 'Yes, it is beautiful,' she agreed, lighting a cigarette. 'Much different from London at this time of the year, I suppose.'

'Oh yes. We're constantly huddling over the fire, wrapped in woollies,' smiled Rachel.

'Is that why you've come back?' asked Irena sharply, and Rachel caught her breath.

'Of course not.'

'No? Then why are you here? André is seeking a divorce. You can't possibly imagine that by coming here you'll change his mind.'

Rachel coloured. 'I didn't imagine any such thing,' she replied hotly.

'But you are here, and that's the point,' remarked Irena coldly. 'Have you met André's future wife?'

'If you mean Leonie Gardner, yes, I have.'

69

'Of course I meant Leonie. André is besotted with her.' She smiled cruelly, enjoying saying those few words. 'I've known Leonie for years. We were at school together.'

'Indeed.' Rachel turned away, pressing a hand to the sick feeling in her stomach.

'Yes. Her parents own a fabulous villa on Lake Cunningham near Nassau. They're very rich, and she's exactly the sort of wife a man like André should have. Not some——' She broke off, as though thinking better of saying what she had in mind, but Rachel swung round.

'Go on,' she demanded tightly. 'Finish it! Not some what?'

'All right, Rachel, I'll tell you.' Irena was breathing heavily. 'Not some penniless, gold-digging little daughter of a man who couldn't keep his hands off a bottle!'

Rachel was horrified. 'It wasn't like that at all,' she cried unevenly.

'Oh, don't give me that!' sneered Irena. 'Of course I am aware that André is attractive, but there was more to it than that. I'm just as amazed as I ever was that he could be so deceived!' She sniffed. 'Anyway, at least he had the sense to get rid of you——'

'That's enough, Irena!' That was Madam Sanchez's voice, as she came silently into the room. 'You will kindly remember that Rachel is our guest, and keep your feelings to yourself.'

'But, Mother——'

'I said that's enough. Good heavens, don't you think we aren't all aware of the difficulties of this situation, but can't we be civilised about it?'

Irena stubbed out her cigarette. 'Why couldn't

André have left her at the hotel in Nassau? Why did he have to bring her here? We're nothing to her, nor she to us.'

'That's not exactly true,' replied André's mother calmly. 'As I said earlier, Rachel became a member of our family when she married André, and as such she will remain, at least so far as I am concerned.'

'Thank you.' Rachel looked gratefully at her mother-in-law.

Irena grimaced. 'Don't you mean she'll remain a drain on our resources?' she enquired rudely. 'Oh, don't bother to answer, I can tell when I'm not wanted!' And with that parting shot she marched out of the room.

After she had gone, Madam Sanchez looked ruefully at Rachel. 'I'm sorry about that, my dear,' she murmured, with a faint smile. 'But Irena never did get on with you, did she? That's why I could never understand why you asked her help to leave André.'

Rachel flushed. 'I suppose because of all of you she was the most likely to help,' she said reflectively. 'Oh, please, don't let's talk about that now. Let's talk about other things. Tell me about Marcus. Where are they at the moment?'

The evening passed by quite pleasantly. Irena ate in her room and the two women were left to themselves. Obviously André had left earlier, and Rachel felt a depressing sense of anti-climax, wondering where he was and who he was with. Mingled with her depression was a trace of jealousy, and while she knew it was stupid and irrational after all that had happened she couldn't help it. Pictures of him with Leonie Gardner kept floating into her head, and she drank rather more than she normally did to dispel the emotions that filled her consciousness. Madam Sanchez followed her suggestions and refrained from questioning her about her personal life, although from time to time Rachel volunteered information about the shop and the interesting exhibitions she had seen in London. Later, they played some music on the hi-fi equipment housed in one corner of the lounge, and it was surfacely pleasant sitting in the velvety evening air, listening to the strains of a piano concerto echoing over their heads.

It wasn't until Rachel was in bed that her fears and recriminations came back to haunt her, but fortunately the wine she had drunk during the course of the evening had made her pleasantly sleepy, and not even her tortuous emotions could prevent her from drifting into dreamless slumber.

CHAPTER FOUR

It was five days before Rachel saw André again.

Actually, she was beginning to get rather restless and anxious about her father, and not even the delights of Maria's company or swimming or sunbathing with Vittorio could compensate her for the anxieties she was feeling. But whenever she broached the subject with either Madam Sanchez or Vittorio she was told to relax and not to worry, and that André would be dealing with everything.

Rachel, curiously enough, didn't doubt that André would deal with everything, but that didn't prevent her from worrying and wondering just how he was setting about it. There were anxieties too about André himself. While she wanted her father extricated somehow from this situation he had got himself into, she didn't want André to implicate himself in any way. It was a strange, unsettling period and she longed to disobey instructions and lift the cream telephone that resided on a table in the lounge and contact somebody—*anybody*!

Vittorio seemed to have been appointed her protector, or perhaps the operative word was gaoler, for he never let her out of his sight, nor did he make any moves towards growing restless, too. Obviously, he had had his instructions and she was expected to follow hers.

But on the morning of the third day she had a visitor. It was Ramon. He had flown over from Palmerina in André's helicopter, and came striding down to the beach where she and Vittorio were lying on the sand. Irena had been prevailed upon to lend Rachel a bathing suit while she was here and Rachel's body was already tanning to a delicious golden brown. Her chestnut hair too had streaks of brightness in it and despite her misgivings about being idle for so long she had never looked better in her life. The rest and relaxation and the good food Madam Sanchez had seen that she ate were working wonders, and Vittorio looked up at his brother rather complacently as he stood regarding them.

'Hello there!' he remarked lazily. 'You look hot, Ramon. You must be working too hard.'

Ramon's face was serious. 'At least no one can say the same about you,' he retorted grimly. 'Hello, Rachel!

Enjoying your holiday?'

Rachel propped herself up on her elbows. 'Thank you, yes.' Then she frowned. 'What's wrong, Ramon? You look very solemn. Have you some news for me?'

Ramon sighed. 'Yes, I've some news, Rachel. Look, we can't talk here. Is there somewhere we can go?'

Vittorio grimaced. 'Take a walk along the beach,' he suggested dryly. 'Don't let me keep you!'

Rachel got to her feet and pulled on a striped beach coat which Irena had also provided, and then stepped over Vittorio's prostrate form to join Ramon. Ramon tucked a hand inside her arm and they walked away along the soft curving line of the beach.

It was another wonderful morning, the sky a deep blue that combined with the sea on the skyline to form an even deeper shade. The white sails of a yacht broke the smooth surface of the ocean, while away in the distance the outline of other islands could be seen. Beside the beach, palm trees grew in abundance, and it was into the shade of these that Ramon took her to talk to her. A log provided a resting place, and Ramon put her on it and then placing one foot on the log he rested his arm on his knee and looked down at her compassionately.

As though sensing that Ramon's news was not good, Rachel said: 'Please. Tell me what it is you have to tell me!' an awful anxiety gripping her suddenly.

Ramon obviously found it difficult to know how to begin, and she said: 'It's—it's my father, isn't it? What's happened? Is he ill? Has he—well, has someone attacked him?' Her eyes were wide and troubled.

Ramon shook his head. 'No one hurt your father,' he said slowly. 'But what I have to say does concern him.

I'm sorry to have to tell you—but he's dead!'

'Dead!' Rachel couldn't take it in. 'You can't be serious!'

'I'm afraid I am.' Ramon sighed. 'Oh, Rachel, I'm sorry to have to be the one to break this news to you, but André isn't here to do it himself.'

Rachel tried to gather her thoughts. 'But why is he dead? What happened?' She licked a tear from the corner of her mouth. 'He—he was perfectly all right when I left.'

Ramon shook his head. 'No, he wasn't, Rachel.'

Rachel stared at him uncomprehendingly. 'What do you mean? Of course he was all right, or I should never have left him!'

Ramon removed his foot from the log and turning seated himself beside her, placing a gentle arm about her shoulders. 'Rachel, your father has been ill for the past year,' he said firmly. 'Now'—he raised a hand—'before you start protesting, I should tell you that doctors have already verified this. He had an incurable disease of the liver, and he had frequently been told that he must stop drinking.' He bent his head. 'But as no doubt you know, he did not.'

'But he didn't drink as much. I—I saw to that.'

'You saw to it when you were there, but how often did your father go out and leave you at times when he could have obtained alcohol?'

Rachel hunched her shoulders. 'He went to race meetings,' she murmured unsteadily.

'Exactly.' Ramon looked at her, brushing another tear from her cheek with the back of his hand. 'Oh, Rachel, don't you see? He sent you here because he knew he was dying. He—he must have known from what the specialists had told him that he hadn't much longer.'

'He saw specialists?' echoed Rachel disbelievingly.

'Yes, yes. That's what I'm trying to tell you, Rachel.'

'But why didn't he tell me? Why didn't he let me share his pain?' she cried passionately.

Ramon shrugged. 'I guess he considered that one way and another he had been enough of a drain on you,' he answered quietly. 'As to the pain, I imagine the barbiturates he was supplied with——' He halted. 'Rachel, you've got to know, his death was the result of barbiturate poisoning.' And as her eyes darkened in dismay, he continued: 'Oh, don't imagine he killed himself. The police don't think it was like that at all. It's a common enough occurrence these days for someone combining alcohol with drugs to inadvertently create poison in their bodies.'

Rachel shuddered and buried her face in her hands. 'Oh, it's terrible! Terrible!' she cried, shaking her head agonisingly. 'Oh, Ramon, what must he have suffered, dying alone like that, with no one to care or to be with him. . . .'

Ramon pressed her close against him. 'I don't suppose for one moment that your father knew anything about it,' he replied softly. 'He was a sick man, aware that his days were numbered. I don't think his death is any more of a tragedy than it might have been had he had to spend months in the incurable ward of some impersonal hospital.'

Rachel cried quietly for several minutes, accepting the handkerchief Ramon handed her and eventually using it to dry her eyes. When she had composed herself a little, she said: 'There—there's things to arrange.' She licked her lips. 'The—the funeral, and so on.' She bit her lip. 'When—when did he die?'

Ramon compressed his lips. 'Actually, Rachel, he died five days ago.'

Rachel stared at him in horror. 'Then he must have died the day after I left England.'

'That's right.'

'But why wasn't I informed? Someone should have contacted me. I left a forwarding address!'

Ramon tried to calm her. 'Listen,' he said firmly. 'Your father was alone in the flat above the shop, wasn't he?'

Rachel nodded, and he continued: 'Four days ago it was Sunday, remember? No one went to the shop, no one tried to get in, no one noticed that there was no one about. Your father must have died on Saturday night, after he got home.'

'He went out?' she asked weakly.

'He was seen in the bar of a nearby hotel just before closing time,' said Ramon heavily.

'Oh no!' she moaned.

'I'm afraid so. At any rate, it wasn't until Monday that the alarm was raised, and by the time they were trying to contact you, André arrived in London.'

'André is in London?' she gasped.

'That's right. He went to help your father, remember?'

Rachel shook her head. 'I never thought he would go himself,' she murmured almost to herself.

Ramon gave a derogatory snort. 'Didn't you? Oh well, he did. And so he was there to deal with everything.' He sighed. 'That's how I got this job. I spent the best part of an hour on the phone to him last night, but he insisted I wait until today to tell you.'

Rachel ran a hand over her forehead in a bewildered fashion. 'I must make arrangements,' she murmured feverishly. 'I've got to get to London myself.'

Ramon shook his head. 'No.'

Now Rachel got unsteadily to her feet, staring at him incredulously. 'What do you mean, *no*?'

'I mean, *no*!' replied Ramon pleasantly. 'Rachel, sit down again. I haven't finished telling you everything.'

Rachel's brows drew together. 'I prefer to stand, and besides, what more could there be?'

Ramon sighed. 'Very well. Your father was buried yesterday.'

Rachel grasped the bole of a tree disbelievingly. 'No!' she said, in horror. 'No, I don't believe you!'

'It's true!'

'No, I don't believe it. You're only telling me that to get me to stay here because André has told you to. They—they couldn't bury *my* father without me being there! It wouldn't be right!'

Ramon stood too, grasping her shoulders. 'Rachel, listen to me, and listen good! Your father had been dead four days when he was buried, and an autopsy had been performed. In addition to which he died of barbiturate poisoning! I hate to be cruel, Rachel, but have you ever seen anybody who died from barbiturate poisoning?'

Rachel choked and wrenched herself away from him, leaning against a tree feeling nauseated. It was incredible, fantastic, impossible! She pressed her fingers to her temples. Only half an hour ago she had been sunbathing on the sand with Vittorio, anxious about her father but secure in the knowledge that André was dealing with his problems for him. And now, only minutes later, she found that the man she had known and loved all her life was dead—and *buried*! It was too cruel! Too inhumane to be true! How could he have kept his illness from her! Why hadn't he confided in her? She had known he had never fully recovered from the death of her mother, but she had hoped that in some way she had compensated him for her mother's loss. But obviously not sufficiently to prevent his weakness from gaining the upper hand.

But what was the most destroying thing about his death was that she had been kept completely apart from it, having no part in it, sharing no last ceremony with his remains. In his usual arrogant, indomitable way, André had used his influence to prevent her being involved. No matter what his reasons had been, and no doubt he would consider he had some, she would never forgive him for this!

Leaning her back against the tree, she turned to look at Ramon. 'How dare André do such a thing?' she cried hysterically. 'He was *my* father. I had a right to be there!'

Ramon shook his head. 'Rachel, I know it's difficult for you to understand now, at this time, but what André has done was for the best, believe me! Your father had a decent burial, and André was there representing you! What more could you have done? Your father was already dead when André arrived. And certainly he wasn't around to care whether or not you attended his funeral! Be sensible, Rachel, for God's sake! Isn't it better to remember your father as you last saw him? As a living, breathing human being, not as a corpse?'

Rachel pressed the palms of her hands to her cheeks. 'I ought to have realised that you would never understand!' she cried bitterly. 'You're one of them, one of the omnipotent few, a *Sanchez*!'

Ramon straightened violently, almost as though she had slapped him. 'Just remember, Rachel, that you are a Sanchez, too,' he reminded her tautly, but Rachel began to shake her head.

'Never,' she gasped wildly, 'never, never, never!' And without another word, she turned and fled back along the beach towards the house.

Rachel sat on the patio of her mother-in-law's house, an unopened magazine in her lap, staring out to sea with concentrated intensity. There was a numbness about her which nothing seemed to erase, and in truth she didn't know whether or not she wanted it erasing. It was two days since Ramon arrived with the terrible news about her father, and although she had got over her hysterical outburst at that horrifying revelation and had accepted the condolences of André's family calmly, nothing really penetrated the shock that still held her in its thrall. Instead, she had withdrawn into herself, realising that to return to England now would accomplish nothing. Her father was dead, and there was absolutely nothing anyone could do about that, and in any case she was virtually a prisoner on Veros until André returned.

Several times Madam Sanchez had attempted to get her to discuss her bereavement in an effort to destroy the shell Rachel had erected about herself, but always Rachel turned aside from it as though it was abhorrent to her and her mother-in-law had been forced to accept her decision. Instead, an uneasy camaraderie prevailed in which life seemed to go on in its normal way, and only beneath the surface did emotions cause undercurrents.

And now it was late afternoon, and Rachel was considering whether she ought to go and take her bath before dinner. Earlier in the afternoon Madam Sanchez had sat on the patio with her, sewing, and carrying on a rather one-sided conversation, until Maria came and claimed her attention and the older woman had agreed to go and supervise Maria's bath as a special treat. In truth, Rachel thought she was glad of the excuse to escape from her daughter-in-law for a while, although she had to admit that Madam Sanchez had treated her with kindness and sympathy and had tried to understand her feelings even though it was difficult in her position.

Suddenly, a strange noise broke the stillness of the air, and Rachel looked up instinctively, seeing the gleaming metal of the silver helicopter approaching swiftly. Immediately her heart skipped a beat, and for the first time since she had heard of her father's death she felt compulsively aware of her surroundings and of her appearance. Getting to her feet, she walked quickly into the house and going to her room she combed her hair into sleek order, smoothed the crispness of the chocolate-coloured dress she was wearing, and applied a small amount of eye make-up. Then, satisfied that she looked cool and composed, she descended the stairs again, slowing as she heard the sound of voices from the lounge. She recognised the tones of Madam Sanchez, and disturbingly, of André, but there was another voice, another feminine voice which she did

81

not recognise.

With determined effort she reached the bottom of the stairs and walked swiftly across to the arched entrance into the lounge, checking in the doorway almost nervously, for the room seemed full of people. But actually, as her eyes surveyed the scene before them she realised that apart from Madam Sanchez and Vittorio, there was only André and the girl, Leonie Gardner, present. Rachel compressed her lips. Why had André brought her here today, now, this moment? Didn't he realise that she would want to talk to him? That she would have things to ask him? To confront him with? Or was that his idea? An attempt to delay an unpleasant interview!

Silence fell on the company as they became aware of her presence, and she stepped into the room uncomfortably, saying: 'Please, don't let me interrupt you.'

André was the first to speak, coming across the room to her with compassionate eyes and attempting to take her hands. But she deliberately put her hands behind her back, her eyes blazing into his, leaving him in no doubt as to her anger.

But André controlled any annoyance at this almost childish display of temper, and said: 'I am so sorry, Rachel. I should have been here myself to break to you the news of your father's death. But it was impossible. I could not be in two places at one and the same time!' He lifted his shoulders in an eloquent gesture. 'Be assured, you have my sympathy!'

Rachel glared at him tremulously. 'Am I supposed to be grateful for that?' she cried, uncaring of the startled glances of the others.

'Rachel...' began Madam Sanchez patiently. 'Not

now!'

Rachel chewed her lower lip. 'I'm sorry, madam,' she said tightly. 'Will you excuse me?' and turning she walked quickly out of the room again.

Once in the hall, she took a deep breath, aware that she was shaking with the force of suppressed emotions. Let André stay with the women, let him protect himself with their presence, sooner or later she would have it out with him.

Fingers suddenly closed cruelly round the flesh of her upper arm, startling her into awareness that she was no longer alone, and her eyes widened when she saw André. 'Come!' he commanded coldly. 'We need to talk!'

Rachel was too startled to protest; besides, this was what she had wanted, wasn't it? Why then did she quiver in his grasp like a frightened insect caught on the pin of an ardent collector? They crossed the hall, and André thrust her through a panelled door which led into a small library. The walls were lined with books and cabinets, and open french windows led on to the patio at the rear of the house. André released his cruel grip on her arm, and crossing to these windows he closed them abruptly.

'Now,' he said, turning, an angry look marring his attractive features, 'what in hell is going on?'

Rachel rubbed her arm mutinously. 'You hurt me!' she accused him coldly.

'Believe me, that's nothing to what I'd like to do when you persist in behaving like a shrewish schoolgirl,' he reviled her mercilessly. 'All right, your father's death has been a terrible shock to you, I'm prepared to accept that, but what I will not accept is this childish behaviour in my mother's house! Kindly keep any outbursts you have to make to me for when we are without witnesses!'

Rachel's cheeks burned. 'I'm sorry if I embarrassed you in front of your future wife!' she muttered scornfully, 'but you really should get rid of one wife before producing another!'

André's hands gripped her shoulders savagely. 'I warn you, Rachel,' he threatened her violently, 'one of these days you will drive me too far!' He thrust her away from him as though he couldn't bear to touch her. 'As for embarrassing me, you ought to know by now that you couldn't do that!'

Rachel's breath came in jerky gulps. For a moment she had been close against his hard body, and her own traitorous emotions had yearned for a closer contact. But the momentary nearness had been in anger, and obviously André had been affected by no such feelings.

Gathering her small store of composure, she said tightly: 'All right, André, let's be civilised about it!' There was sarcasm in her voice. 'I won't push you, if you don't push me!' She bent her head. 'And now I think you've evaded your responsibilities long enough.'

'What do you mean?' He was suspicious.

'I'll explain,' said Rachel tautly. 'You accuse me of behaving childishly. Well, maybe the reason I do is because you treat me like a child!' She took a deep breath, staring at him accusingly.

André moved indolently. 'What is that supposed to mean?' he asked harshly. 'All I can imagine you are meaning are my actions regarding your father's death and subsequent burial.'

'Oh, how cold you are!' she gasped, unable to prevent herself. 'My father's death and subsequent burial!' She caught her breath on a sob. 'You make it sound like an office memo!'

André gave an impatient exclamation. 'For God's sake, Rachel! What do you want me to say?' He raked a hand through his thick hair. 'I'm sorry he's dead, you must know that, but it wasn't by my hand he died!'

'At least he won't be a drain on your resources any longer,' cried Rachel bitterly, fighting back the tears that threatened behind her eyes.

André sighed heavily. 'Hell, Rachel, don't bring up everything I said about him! Maybe I was a bit harsh, but good heavens, I didn't know the man was dying, did I?'

Rachel turned away. 'But when he was dead, you made pretty damn sure he had no chance to trouble you longer than was necessary,' she imputed him scornfully.

André uttered an expletive. 'That's a pretty filthy thing to say,' he said bleakly, and Rachel wished she could see his face. His voice had sounded shaken, as though her words had got through to him cuttingly.

She bent her head. 'Can you deny it?' she asked quietly.

André did not reply and she swung round to see him reaching for a decanter of brandy from the tray on the bureau near by. He poured himself several measures and swallowed half of it at a gulp. Then he turned to look at her, the decanter and glass still in his hands.

'So that's what you think?' he ground out harshly. 'You think I had your father buried without your attendance for some nefarious purposes of my own, is that it?'

Rachel did not reply, and he went on: 'All right, Rachel, I'll tell you something. Have you ever seen a body that's been dead of barbiturate poisoning for several days? Have you ever seen a rotting mass of flesh that was once a living, breathing human being whom you had known and loved?'

Rachel stared at him with pained eyes, and then pressed her hands to her ears. 'Don't!' she cried, in agony. 'Don't!'

'Why not? That's what you want to hear, isn't it? You wanted to be a party to all the sordid details. Well, I can give them to you. Do you want to know the results of the post-mortem? Do you want to know in what state of decay your father's liver really was? Do you want——'

'Stop it! Stop it! You're cruel, *cruel*!' She sank down into a chair, burying her face in her hands.

'No, Rachel,' he said heavily, finishing his drink. 'I'm not cruel! If I'd been cruel I'd have wired you, knowing that if you came to London you would be forced to look at your father if only because you felt you should. I saved you that necessity by taking the whole responsibility for it on myself! But you can't see that, can you? All you can see is another example of the arrogance of the Sanchez clan, isn't that right!'

Rachel felt the hot tears forcing themselves between her fingers and did not reply. She was suddenly aware of the death of her father in all its morbid detail, and while there was resentment at André's assumption of responsibility, there was a kind of relief, too, that she had not been subjected to such a harrowing ordeal.

When she looked up, after drying her eyes, she found him standing by the french windows, smoking a cigar

and staring out thoughtfully. Sniffing a little, she got to her feet.

'I suppose I ought to have been grateful,' she said chokily, still near to tears.

André looked at her sardonically. 'Oh no, Rachel,' he said chillingly. 'That would have been too much!'

Ignoring his coldness, she said: 'What—what about the shop? I mean—the reason I came here in the first place! Did—did you see the police? Or the men?' She bit her lip hard to prevent it trembling.

André tapped ash into a tray. Then he sighed. 'Rachel, I don't think there were any men. Certainly the police had heard nothing about it. They never called at the shop. A superintendent assured me of that.'

Rachel's eyes were wide. 'What!' she gasped.

André shrugged. 'Can't you see the pattern?' he enquired rather wearily. 'There were no men! He wasn't in trouble of any kind, except of the most personal kind.' He shook his head. 'Look, Rachel, he knew if anything happened to him, you'd be alone in the world, and London can be a pretty frightening place for any young woman who has no one to turn to.'

Rachel felt bewildered. 'I don't understand,' she exclaimed, putting a hand to her head.

André studied the glowing tip of his cigar. 'Rachel, he sent you here to find me because he knew with me you'd be safe! Secure! He knew that if anything happened to him before you contacted me, you never would after he was dead. He had to devise some plan to get you to come out here, and the only way he could do that was for him to be in trouble, real trouble, trouble of a kind you would be unable to handle. He knew if he suggested you coming out here in the ordinary way, you'd veto the plan, so he used his brain, and tricked you into coming.'

Rachel shook her head disbelievingly. 'I can't believe it!' she exclaimed, 'it's not possible!' She bit her lip harder. 'Why should he do such a thing? I'm perfectly capable of taking care of myself!'

'Well, obviously he didn't think so. Rachel, he knew he was dying, and he knew he hadn't much time left to get you to come out here. I think it was a pretty clever plan!'

Rachel stared at him. 'But why should he send me to you?' She turned away. 'He knew our marriage was over.'

'Yes.' André studied her bent head. 'He knew more than you did, Rachel.'

'What do you mean?'

André withdrew a letter from his pocket, and tapped it on his palm. 'This was the letter my solicitors mailed to you several weeks ago.'

Rachel's lips parted. 'Oh no!'

'Oh yes. Your father knew I was seeking a divorce. He knew he hadn't a moment to lose.'

Rachel moved restlessly, getting to her feet and walking unsteadily across the room. 'Oh, how could he have done such a thing!' she said bitterly, shaking her head. 'Oh, how could he?' Her voice broke on a sob.

André came across to her. 'Oughtn't you to be grateful he did?' he asked, rather roughly. 'You couldn't have handled everything yourself. You needed someone— some man, and I'm the only man you should turn to!'

'You!' She stared at him through tear-wet lashes. 'Why you? You don't want me? You've got Leonie!

88

You want a divorce, remember?'

André's eyes darkened, and his gaze lingered on her mouth, her lips parted and trembling. 'All right,' he said, rather tautly, 'I want a divorce. But that doesn't mean we have to be uncivilised about it. You're still a member of this family. Like my mother says, you're a Sanchez!'

Rachel shook her head. 'I'm not. I'm Rachel Jardin!'

'You're Rachel Sanchez!' announced André harshly, 'and I for one will not let you forget it!'

'What will you do?' she taunted him shakily.

'I have plans for you,' he replied quietly, 'and you will do as your father wanted and follow them!'

'The shop——'

'The shop has been taken care of. Oh, don't worry, I haven't sold it over your head, but you needn't trouble about it for a while.'

'And if I disagree?'

'You'll be destitute. You've no money, on your own admission, you've no money, and I won't pay another cent into your London bank!'

'I—I could sue you!'

'And I could produce a dozen witnesses to prove that you've committed adultery, and that my divorce requires no arrangements for alimony!'

Rachel hunched her shoulders. She felt defeated. 'You're a brute!' she said unevenly. 'I hate you, André Sanchez!'

'You'll say that once too often, Rachel,' he muttered angrily, and without another word he brushed past her and opening the door went out, slamming it behind him.

CHAPTER FIVE

THAT evening Rachel dressed for dinner with extra care. The maid had informed her that Mr. André and Miss Gardner were staying for dinner, and although Rachel knew it was ridiculous she had no intention of allowing Leonie Gardner the satisfaction of looking down on her appearance. Her clothes might not be as expensive as Leonie's, but they were plain and elegant, and she knew she had good dress sense. She had brought two evening dresses with her in case she was expected to dress for dinner at the hotel, and now she chose the second of these, an ankle-length gown of apricot-patterned silk. It was styled like a caftan, with an upstanding collar dipping to a low vee in front, and the sleeves were wide and feminine. Her chestnut hair was soft as silk against her neck, and the sun had touched her skin to honey. Despite her grief over her father, there was a haunting beauty about her, accentuating the slightly slanted wideness of her eyes. The knowledge gave her an added confidence, although she was sure she would fade into insignificance beside Leonie's classical fairness.

She went down to the lounge just before the appointed time for the meal, and found Vittorio and Irena, André and Leonie, and Madam Sanchez, all taking cocktails together. Obviously, Leonie and André had not been able to change and Leonie was still wearing the navy blue Crimplene suit she had been wearing when Rachel had seen her so briefly during the afternoon. Her cool blue eyes surveyed

Rachel condescendingly, and obviously she did not particularly like what she saw. This time Vittorio took charge of the situation, coming forward to draw Rachel into the group and asking her whether she would like a cocktail. His admiring eyes were a balm to her tortured spirit, and she bestowed a warm smile upon him as she took his arm and accompanied him across to the cocktail cabinet. Vittorio gave her a strange glance and as he poured her drink, he said:

'You're looking so much better, Rachel! Do you feel better?'

Rachel lifted her shoulders expressively. 'I think I do,' she murmured, taking her drink. 'In any event, I feel more able to face whatever is to come!' She sipped her cocktail thoughtfully, allowing her eyes to survey the room over the rim of her glass.

Madam Sanchez came across to them. 'What a pretty dress, Rachel,' she commented gently, a smile in her eyes. 'Has Vittorio been telling you how attractive you look?'

Vittorio smiled wryly. 'Hardly,' he remarked, glancing expressively at André, and Madam Sanchez gave him a quelling stare.

'Tell me, Rachel,' she said, changing the subject, 'has André been able to reassure you about—well—everything?'

Rachel bent her head, fingering the rim of her glass. 'I think André has removed the numbness,' she said honestly. 'Somehow I can accept it a little better now.'

Madam Sanchez pressed her arm. 'Oh, I'm so glad, my dear. I hated to see you so downcast. Now come along and meet Leonie. I'm sure you've never been properly introduced.'

Rachel hesitated, and then accompanied Madam Sanchez across to where André, Leonie, and Irena were talking together. Irena looked annoyed at their intrusion, but she said nothing, and if André too was annoyed he disguised it admirably. Leonie's eyes flickered slightly, and, deliberately Rachel thought, she slid a hand inside André's arm, her fingers gently caressing his.

'Rachel, my dear, this is Leonie!' Madam Sanchez smiled her introduction. 'Leonie, you mustn't mind Rachel being here. Naturally, she and I are great friends, and it was right that she should come to André with her problems.'

Leonie's lips thinned. 'Naturally,' she murmured, almost inaudibly, then she looked up at André. 'Darling, when dinner is over, we aren't staying, are we?' She squeezed his arm. 'I mean—you know we promised Mom and Dad to dine there this evening.' She gave a slight sigh. 'Of course, I understood that you had business to attend to here, and that your mother wanted to see you, but after dinner, we really should go.' She stroked his lapel with her other hand. 'After all, you've neglected me dreadfully being away so long, and we have things to talk about.'

André's lean features were serious and he didn't respond to her playful tactics. 'I'm sorry, Leonie, but after dinner I have to talk to Rachel. There are things to arrange.'

Rachel, who had listened to Leonie's appeal, gave an almost impatient flick to her gown and turned to Madam Sanchez. 'I really ought to apologise for staying here so long,' she said quietly. 'Naturally now I shall be making arrangements to go back to England.' She ignored André's swiftly indrawn breath, and continued: 'I—I can easily get a job. I'm still quite an efficient book-keeper, and I have my library training——'

'You're going to South America,' said André, behind her, and she swung round in astonishment.

'South America!' she echoed, and even Leonie looked astounded.

'Yes, South America; Brazil to be exact,' returned André bleakly. 'Since you insist on conducting your arguments in public!' His eyes belied the anger he was holding in check, and Rachel shivered.

'I don't understand,' she said, rather tremulously.

'Nor do I!' exclaimed Irena, joining in for the first time. 'Just what kind of arrangements are you making, André?'

André gave her a killing glance. 'While I was in London I saw Marcus and Olivia. You knew they were there as well as I did. Marcus has to return to the Rio office sooner than he expected, and he and Olivia are flying directly there from London, instead of stopping off here for Maria. Rachel will accompany Maria, and Tottie of course, to Rio.'

Rachel shook her head in amazement. 'You expect me to agree to it, just like that!' she exclaimed weakly.

André's eyes were dark. 'Right now you have no choice,' he replied, daring her to argue with him yet again.

Rachel finished her drink and walked dazedly over to Vittorio by the cabinet. 'Give me another,' she said unsteadily, and frowning, he did as she asked. After she had swallowed half of her second drink he offered her a cigarette and she took it gratefully, inhaling the nicotine deeply, and trying to assimilate what she had just heard.

There was little doubt that if André had made up his mind she would do as he asked, and in any case it was the least she could do for the family after Madam Sanchez had been so kind, but what was behind it all? What plans was he contemplating for her? What was his ultimate intention? Did he hope she might meet someone, some other member of his family in Brazil, and thus free him from his obligations by marrying again herself? She knew there were distant cousins in Rio whom Marcus worked with, and it was not inconceivable that André should be so despotic as to imagine he could arrange her life so callously.

Luckily the maid came at that moment to announce that dinner was served, and the informality of the meal, plus the fact that she was seated beside Vittorio on Madam Sanchez's right hand, gave Rachel some respite. But she ate little, picking disinterestedly at her food, conscious all the while of the man across the table and the concentrated efforts his companion was making to monopolise his attention. Seeing André's dark head bent often in Leonie's direction disturbed Rachel more than she cared to admit, and to imagine them alone together, possibly making love, was distasteful to her. And it was obvious from the way Leonie worshipped him with her eyes that she would be unable to deny him anything. Rachel's nails bit into the palms of her hands. This was what her father had sent her out here to find—but why? What streak of cruelty had made him thrust her into André's life again at a time when he so obviously did not want to see her?

When dinner was over, and they all adjourned to

the lounge for coffee, Rachel found André beside her. 'I want to talk to you,' he said in a low voice, without any trace of animosity.

Rachel was aware that Leonie, seated with Irena on the divan, was watching them closely, and with deliberate archness, she said: 'Ought you to be neglecting Leonie? I understood she wanted to leave directly after dinner.'

André's blue eyes blazed with suppressed annoyance. 'Rachel, for God's sake, couldn't you just come with me without creating a scene?'

Rachel glanced expressively across at Leonie. 'I'm not creating a scene,' she disclaimed charmingly. 'But someone else might!'

André took a deep breath. 'Leonie knows I have to talk to you,' he replied evenly. 'She has no reason to feel jealous!'

Rachel flinched at the cutting cruelty of his observation, and some unwarranted devil of injustice inside her longed to make him eat those arrogant words. With a casual lift of her head, she said calmly: 'Very well then, André.'

André thust his hands into the pockets of his trousers. 'We'll go to the library,' he said, indicating that she should precede him out of the room.

But Rachel halted, shaking her head. 'But it's such a lovely night, André. I'd prefer to walk outside.'

André studied her expression searchingly. 'The library, I think,' he commanded softly.

Rachel smiled sardonically. 'What's the matter, André? Are you afraid Leonie might object if we walked in the garden?'

André shook his head. 'Not at all,' he replied indifferently. 'And if it means so much to you...'

Rachel dug the nails of one hand into the palm of the other, refusing to retaliate in the way he expected her to. Instead, she walked ahead of him out of the room, and across the tiled hall.

Outside, the night air was scented with the perfumes of the many flowers Madam Sanchez cultivated in her garden. She had introduced many English varieties to the rich soil around her villa, and stocks mingled with the more exotic scents of hibiscus and magnolia.

Now Rachel halted and turned to find André behind her. 'It's a beautiful night,' she said, in an effort to break the silence that had fallen.

André lifted his shoulders eloquently. 'The silence used to bore you, if I remember correctly,' he remarked bleakly. 'Shall we go through here?'

Rachel compressed her lips and followed him through an arched trellis to where the formal gardens of the house fell away towards the beach. Several yards from the house, he stopped and said:

'I think this is far enough, don't you?'

Rachel shrugged, and he took her silence as agreement, and drew out some papers which he tapped on his hand. 'Everything you need is here,' he said coolly. 'Passport, documents, everything.'

'I have my passport,' returned Rachel sharply.

'Yes, I know. This is Maria's. You leave the day after tomorrow, a flight from Nassau in the afternoon. Marcus or Olivia will meet you at Galeao. They'll take it from there. Clothes—that kind of thing—can be bought in Nassau tomorrow. Ramon will look after you.'

Rachel felt almost stunned by his cool assumption of

her acceptance. 'You've worked everything out, haven't you?' she exclaimed bitterly. 'Just how long am I expected to stay in Brazil?'

André frowned, his face vaguely visible in the lights that emanated from the house into the garden. 'I suggested perhaps three months,' he remarked casually. 'Olivia will be glad of your company. Marcus is a busy man these days and doesn't have a lot of free time. Besides, it will enable you to recover completely from your bereavement in surroundings that are strange and therefore impersonal.'

Rachel shook her head incredulously. 'Your overbearing arrogance never fails to astound me!' she cried passionately. 'And what about your divorce?' Her tone was bitter. 'Won't this hold up the proceedings?'

André shook his head, putting the papers back in his pocket. 'I don't foresee any difficulties there,' he replied coldly. 'Your agreement isn't necessary in the circumstances. You left me, remember, and desertion requires less than five years to be made absolute!'

'You've got it all worked out, haven't you?' she exclaimed hotly. 'And such a convenient arrangement to get rid of me!'

André's eyes darkened. 'That was not my intention, and you know it!' he snapped, caught on the raw. 'You were quite prepared to return to London. My plans for you were made in an attempt to ease your grief!'

Rachel kicked a stone impatiently. 'Why is it you're always right, and I'm always wrong?' she asked angrily. 'I always misunderstand your most generous motives, don't I?' Her tone was scornful.

André took a step towards her. 'You deliberately provoke violence!' he snapped harshly.

Rachel gave a scornful laugh. 'From you?' she asked mockingly. 'How could I do that? You're safe and secure behind your mistress's skirts!'

But now she realised she had gone too far and the look in his eyes terrified her. She really thought he could have killed her in that moment. With stumbling steps, she turned and ran away from him, down the slope through the lawns and rose gardens, through the small ranch fencing on to the beach. She wasn't aware that he was following her, she only knew she must escape from the primitive fury in his eyes. After all, he had Spanish blood in his veins, and the Spaniards could be very cruel. It wasn't until she turned to take a breath that she realised her own panting passage had silenced the sound of his pursuit, and he was right behind her.

A choking sob broke from her lips and she sped along the beach, holding up the hampering skirts of her gown in an effort to escape retribution. But he was swifter, and stronger, and infinitely more powerful, and he caught a handful of her hair, halting her in an agonised scream, and causing her to sink to her knees before him. Tears sprang to her eyes as much from the pain of her head as from fear of him and anger still had the upper hand.

'You pig!' she cried, putting a hand to her head, her face pale and tear-wet in the moonlight.

André stood above her, legs apart, the epitome of male dominance, and she tried unsteadily to get to her feet. But André's eyes blazed with unleashed passion, and when she tried to move he came down beside her, pressing her back on to the sand, her hands pinned behind her head.

'Brute, bully; let go of me!' she cried, twisting her head from side to side as he stared down at her, his face only inches above hers. But then something in his eyes made her stop struggling and her breath became a thunder in her ears as all resistance went out of her.

'God, oh God!' she heard him groan agonisingly, and then the hard pressure of his mouth sought the parted sweetness of hers, and the whole weight of his hard body obliterated coherent thought. Rachel's arms slid round his neck, her fingers in his hair pressing his head closer as her body arched against his. 'Rachel, Rachel,' he muttered feverishly, searching her eyes and ears and throat with burning lips. 'You're driving me out of my mind!' His mouth sought hers again. Her whole being was on fire for him; no one could make love like André, and nothing mattered but that he should go on and on . . .

The sound of voices along the beach brought André to his senses, and with a savage ejaculation he got abruptly to his feet, brushing sand from the immaculate material of his suit, and smoothing his hair into some semblance of order. He stood looking down at her with inflamed eyes, and then said: 'Get up, for heaven's sake!' and bending, wrenched her to her feet.

Rachel looked at him uncomprehendingly, and he said harshly: 'Don't imagine this changes anything, Rachel!' in a low tone.

Rachel felt as though a douche of cold water had been scattered over her. Stiffening her shoulders, she said: 'You're flattering yourself, Mr. Sanchez!' in a scornful voice. She brushed her gown into place, aware that nothing would restore order to the wild disarray of her hair, and she could only hope that no one would notice, or if they did that they would put it down to the wind. She couldn't imagine who would have followed them anyway, but she managed to stroll casually at André's side back to the lights of the house that spread a glow over one stretch of the sands, ignoring the speculative glances he cast in her direction.

Leonie, Irena, and Vittorio were standing just inside the gardens and all turned to look at Rachel and André as they came to join them. Rachel had to admire André's nonchalance, as he said calmly: 'What's going on? Is this a search-party? I assure you we have only been a few yards along the beach. Rachel' —he hesitated infinitesimally—'wanted to get some air.'

Leonie came to his side at once. 'Darling, it's getting late. We really must go.'

André bent his head in assent. 'Okay, Leonie, right now! I'll just go and see my mother before we leave.'

'All right, darling.' Leonie let him go and André walked swiftly into the house. Then Rachel became the cynosure of all eyes, and she was glad of the anonymity of the moonlight. No heated cheeks could be noticed, and hers were heated, she was sure. In fact, there was an awful sense of anti-climax about the whole evening, and a disturbing ache in the lower region of her stomach. Some wild emotion inside her cried out for fulfilment, and she wondered what André would say if she begged him to stay, in front of his so-elegant girl-friend. His touch, his lovemaking, even his anger, had awakened all the latent longings inside her, desires which she had thought stilled with the passage of time but which now she knew were not stilled at all. She wanted André back, there was no sense in denying the futility of the knowledge, and that he was to leave in a few minutes was something she could not accept.

Uncaring of what construction the others might place on her actions, she turned and ran up the paths into the house and encountered André in the hall on the point of leaving. He would have passed her, but she caught his arm impulsively, preventing him. 'André,' she murmured huskily, allowing her fingers to caress the smooth texture of his sleeve.

André's breathing was uneven, but he said roughly: 'What do you want of me now, Rachel?'

Rachel ran her tongue over her lower lip. 'André,' she said softly, 'we've got to talk.'

André's eyes narrowed. 'Don't try anything, Rachel,' he snapped violently. 'Not now.'

Rachel touched his cheek with her fingertips. 'André,' she repeated pleadingly, 'don't go like this! Not in anger! Just now—out there—you wanted me——'

André stared at her with glazed eyes. 'Yes,' he snarled harshly, 'I want you, but by God! I'll never take you!' He thrust her away from him.

Rachel's eyes mirrored her hurt. 'Why?' she asked unsteadily.

André raked a hand through his hair. 'I loved you, Rachel,' he ground out fiercely. 'To distraction! I never thought I'd ever get you out of my mind, but I have, and now I've found somebody who loves me in the way I used to love you, and I find it's a far more acceptable arrangement! Oh, I admit you're a beautiful woman, a beautiful desirable woman as you ever were, but while I might desire your body, I want no part of your soul, and that's what love is all about, so the poets say.'

Rachel shook her head in bitterness. 'You're a cruel swine, André,' she gasped. 'You never used to be so cruel.'

'I'm the way you made me,' he bit out the words. 'Once my life wasn't good enough for you, you were bored and restless, so bored and restless that you deliberately destroyed the child—*my child*—you were carrying!'

'That's not true!' she cried weakly. 'It wasn't like that at all. I didn't want to lose the baby—I wanted it!'

André looked scornful and disbelieving. 'You must have said that to yourself so many times you almost believe it yourself!' he sneered.

'It's the truth!'

'Then why did you run away afterwards? You could have had other children.'

Rachel stared at him incredulously. '*You* ask me that!' she exclaimed. 'After all you said—after the way you acted!'

'So it was my fault?' André turned away. 'Goodnight, Rachel. Happy trip!' and with that he left her.

Rachel stumbled into the lounge, pausing nauseated on the threshold, and looked straight into Madam Sanchez's compassionate eyes.

'You heard?' she whispered wearily.

Madam Sanchez nodded. 'Yes, I heard, Rachel. Come and sit down. I think it's time we had a talk, don't you?'

Rachel lifted her shoulders helplessly, but although she couldn't see what good talking would do, she did not relish the prospect of returning to her room and allowing her tortuous thoughts to destroy her. So she advanced slowly into the lounge and accepted the drink André's mother thrust into her hand. She knew she must look pretty dreadful; she had felt the blood drain out of her face as André spoke to her, and now she felt completely enervated.

Madam Sanchez indicated that she should sit on the divan and then seated herself opposite her. Rachel sipped the brandy she had been given, and tried to think coherently. But the memory of André's cruel lashing words remained, and she shivered in spite of the heat of her body. Eventually Irena returned, and she came to the lounge door, viewing her mother and her sister-in-law mockingly.

'What is this?' she asked sneeringly. 'Confession?'

Madam Sanchez gave her daughter a quelling glance. 'If you have nothing constructive to say, Irena, kindly keep your comments to yourself,' she snapped.

Irena shrugged, viewing Rachel curiously. 'What's wrong? Has André given Rachel the thrashing she deserves?'

Rachel looked up at Irena, anger temporarily banishing her pain. 'You're always so interested in other people's problems, aren't you, Irena?' she flared. 'Why, I wonder? Is it because that's what life has become for you? An ever-changing panorama of which you are just the spectator? Because that's all you are—a spectator!' Her voice broke ignominiously, and she bent her head, fighting for control.

Irena gave a self-satisfied smile. 'Well, well, something's happened, that's for sure! I've never seen you cry before, Rachel. It's quite a novelty. I understood witches couldn't cry.'

'Irena!' Madam Sanchez was incensed. 'Leave the room! Your behaviour appals me! Have you no feelings whatsoever?'

Irena turned to her mother. 'Why are you defending her? André is your son as well as my brother and she attempted to ruin his life! Thank heavens, he's had the sense to find someone suitable at last!'

'Irena! Must I repeat myself?' Madam Sanchez rose to her feet. 'I warn you——'

'All right, all right!' Irena turned back to the door. 'I'll go, and leave you to your confidences. But don't let her fool you, Mother. She's completely ruthless when it comes to getting what she wants!'

Madam Sanchez raised her hand impatiently, but Irena was gone, climbing the stairs, whistling tunelessly to herself. Madam Sanchez seated herself again and looked at Rachel who was trying to drink her brandy while her hand shook uncontrollably. There was compassion in her gaze, and Rachel felt self-pity welling up inside her again. But she fought it back, and shaking her head, said, as casually as she could: 'Silly, isn't it, but women were always illogical creatures!'

Madam Sanchez compressed her lips, and then reaching out a hand she put it over Rachel's which lay in her lap. 'Rachel, Rachel,' she said slowly. 'You don't have to act with me. I thought we understood one another.'

Rachel ran her tongue over her upper lip. 'Oh, how can we understand one another?' she cried hopelessly. 'We're on separate sides. We always were. That was why——' She halted abruptly.

'Why—you couldn't come to see me before leaving

André?' asked Madam Sanchez shrewdly.

'That's right.' Rachel bent her head. 'I wanted to. I needed someone to confide in, but somehow it was impossible to turn to you—André's mother.'

'I can see that,' nodded Madam Sanchez. 'And I suppose Irena was only too willing to assist you to leave.'

Rachel sighed. 'Of course she was. At the time I was grateful, but now . . .' Her voice trailed away. Then she looked up. 'Did—did André explain what my father did?'

Madam Sanchez nodded. 'Yes, he told me. I think your father was a rather courageous man, don't you?'

Rachel spread her hands. 'Oh, I suppose so, I shall miss him terribly. I loved him very much. But I can't understand why he should have thought it necessary to send me here—to André—when he knew he was seeking a divorce.'

'Can't you? Well, perhaps he thought he had not a moment to lose, and in the event he was right.'

'Yes, but I would have managed. I'm not one of those helpless females. Maybe if I had been, André and I would have made a success of our marriage.'

Madam Sanchez frowned. 'And you think your marriage was not a success?'

'How can you ask such a question?' exclaimed Rachel.

Madam Sanchez studied her pale face. 'Your marriage broke down, so you say it failed,' she commented quietly. 'But there was a time when you believed it a success.'

Rachel bit her lip. 'Of course—in the beginning . . .'

'Yes, in the beginning, when André brought you to

the Bahamas after your honeymoon. You were happy then, weren't you?' Rachel nodded slowly, and Madam Sanchez continued: 'And because this was so, my son became afraid for his happiness!'

She sighed, spreading her hands expressively. 'Rachel you found it hard to understand the strains placed on a man in André's position. He has enemies, he knows this, but you, from your quiet, uneventful background, could not see the dangers.'

Rachel shook her head. 'He was so possessive!'

Madam Sanchez raised her dark eyebrows. 'And it got worse?'

'Yes.' Rachel nodded.

'Let me try and explain. André loved you when he married you, but it is not until you have lived with someone that you really begin to feel you could not live without them. This was André's trouble. His love for you developed as the months went by, and with it his possessiveness, his almost frantic anxiety that nothing should ever harm you.'

Rachel ran a hand over her forehead. 'Why did he never try to explain? Why was he always so definite that he was right and I was wrong? He never attempted to understand how I felt.'

'Did you attempt to understand how he felt?' asked his mother softly.

Rachel sighed. Could she say she had, in all honesty? With jerky movements she reached for a cigarette, and after it was lit, she said: 'Even so, loving someone does not give you the right to dominate that person so that their lives are just a pale shadow of your own.'

'I agree. André is a dominant personality, and with you he lost perspective. Nevertheless, it was love that drove you away, Rachel, not hate.'

Rachel drew deeply on her cigarette. 'Did André talk to you about—about the baby?'

Madam Sanchez folded her hands. 'You talk to me,' she urged gently. 'Let us talk about that time.'

Rachel heaved a sigh. It was still difficult, even after all this time, to talk about it. But she realised Madam Sanchez only wanted to help her, and it would do her good to discuss it with a woman. There had never been anyone she could confide in. She sought about for words to begin, and finally said carefully: 'André thought my restlessness was founded on boredom. It wasn't. Life with André could never be boring. But I did object to the confinement, even though in retrospect I realise my behaviour was childish and irresponsible.'

'André told you about Lilaine?' queried Madam Sanchez quietly.

'No. Vittorio told me. I don't know what to say to demonstrate the horror I felt when he told me. It must have been terrible for you.'

'Yes, it was.' Madame Sanchez sighed. 'It was terrible for André, too. After all, it was confirmation of his anxieties in a way.'

'I know. But you must realise it is not a commonplace occurrence.'

'Agreed. But, Rachel, when you love somebody as André loved you, you don't take *any* chances.'

Rachel lifted her shoulders. 'I had to wait and worry when André was away,' she pointed out.

'André is a man. I suppose he thought his chances were better, but after some of the terrible things you hear nowadays, one wonders whether one has any reason for believing such a thing.' She half smiled. 'But come, we are digressing. Go on about your reasons for leaving.'

Rachel found it difficult to go on. Her brain spun in the effort to think clearly and lucidly, and Madam Sanchez's words of explanation did nothing to ease her unhappiness.

At last she swallowed, and said: 'André said if I had a baby I'd have less time to cause trouble!' She sighed. 'That's exactly how he put it, during a row we had!' She chewed her lower lip. 'You—you can't imagine how I felt when he said that! Until then, *I'd* wanted a baby, but André had said we needed time to be alone together.'

'He was jealous,' remarked Madam Sanchez calmly. 'He wanted nothing and no one to distract you from him.'

'But wasn't that selfish?' pleaded Rachel desperately. 'My reasons for having a baby were possessive, too. But I wanted part of André inside me! I wanted to feel his baby kicking in my stomach and know that whatever happened I would have his child!' Her impassioned voice quietened. She drew on her cigarette. 'Anyway, I said no, then. When he threw the idea at me, I said that nothing would induce me to give him more of a hold over me!' Her voice broke and she had to compose herself before she could go on. 'Any—anyway, as you know, I did become pregnant. Of course we had made up our quarrel. I could never resist André if he really set his mind to it, and he knew it. But when I found I was pregnant, I accused him of taking advantage of me, and we had another row. Oh, it was terrible!' She buried her face in her hands, and Madam

Sanchez rose to her feet and leaving her alone crossed to the french doors that opened on to the veranda. She stood there for a while, giving Rachel time to recompose herself, and then returned to her seat when Rachel looked up, wiping her eyes vigorously.

'I'm sorry,' said Rachel self-consciously. 'But it's not easy.'

'No, I realise that,' replied André's mother gently. 'Do you want to go on?'

'Oh yes. Now I've started, I'll tell you everything.' Rachel sniffed. 'Well—afterwards, after this row, we became civil with one another again, but André never touched me, never slept with me, after that. He—he—moved his clothes into the spare room, and although outwardly things looked the same, underneath it was awful!' She sighed. 'I was hurt at first, too hurt to retaliate, but later my temper got the better of me, I'm afraid, and I started to be unco-operative and silent when he was around. Ramon came often to visit us, as you know. I think he enjoyed my company, and I enjoyed his, in a purely platonic way, of course. I didn't tell him about the baby. I suppose I should have done, but I didn't want to talk about the thing that had caused this rift between André and me.' She looked into Madam Sanchez's eyes. 'Can you understand how I felt? Can you?'

André's mother frowned. 'I'm beginning to. Go on, Rachel.'

'Oh well, Ramon used to take me out for days, swimming and fishing and so on, and I continued to accompany him. Then, one trip, *the* trip, we went skin-diving.' She hunched her shoulders. 'I know I got breathless as I went down, and I felt this awful choking feeling. I told Ramon I was going up, you know—by gestures, and he followed me. But I think the continued exertion of so many sporting activities had got the better of me, and I felt weak and shaky. Ramon brought me home, but the damage was done.' She gave a cynical shrug of her shoulders. 'No grand gestures, no dramatic scene, just a miscarriage that was agony, both physical and mental.'

'Did you tell all this to André?'

Rachel gave a mirthless laugh. 'Do you imagine he would have listened? Oh, no, when he came home and found the doctor in attendance, he was in no mood for conversation.' She sighed. 'Besides, I was in no fit state to be coherent, myself. You won't believe this, but I wanted that baby, really wanted it! Oh, I said all sorts of things to André, but it was pure and utter stupidity on my part that made me act that way, I see that now. Afterwards, when André could see me, could talk to me, he accused me of deliberately attempting to bring a miscarriage upon myself. I was too weak to disagree with him. It was no good anyway. He never wanted to see me again. That was his attitude!'

Madam Sanchez clucked her tongue. 'But, child, couldn't you see that he was hurt, terribly hurt? Didn't it occur to you that his anger was directed as much against himself as at you for causing you to have to suffer this terrible thing? In all this, you seem to have lost sight of the fact that André *loved* you. You might hurt him, cause him agonies of self-recrimination, but he still loved you.'

Rachel stared at her. 'How can you say that?' she gasped.

'Because I know what he was like when you left!'

retorted André's mother sharply. 'He was like a man demented! Twice he came to London to see you, and twice he returned without attempting to do so.'

'What?'

'Of course. Do you think he let you go without ascertaining that you were safe and well? Both times he saw your father, but of course, your father was prevailed upon not to tell you.'

Rachel was speechless for a moment, then she said: 'It seems my father has kept many things to himself,' she murmured bitterly. 'Why didn't André want me to know?'

'Your father told him you were still very depressed. That you were only slowly recovering from your illness, and that André's appearance might create more difficulties for you. In return, André made your father promise that if at any time you were in doubt or should need him, he would contact André immediately. I suppose that was why your father sent you to André now.'

Rachel shook her head, still slightly bewildered. 'I see,' she said huskily. 'And now it's too late!'

Madam Sanchez rose to her feet and sighed. 'Yes. André is to marry Leonie. She will make him a good and dutiful wife, I have no doubts about that. What troubles me is whether André will make her a good and dutiful husband.'

'What do you mean?' Rachel looked up at her.

Madam Sanchez shrugged her shoulders. 'I heard you with André in the hall, remember,' she said quietly. 'Though he may never admit it, you are not out of his system yet.' She turned to Rachel with a half-smile. 'Oh, Rachel, what problems we create for ourselves!'

Rachel bent her head in silent assent.

The older woman sighed again. 'Ah, well, child, you are going to Rio, with Maria, and I cannot say I am not glad. It will do you the world of good to get away from everything you have known for a while. And the weather there is marvellous at this time of the year. Marcus's house is near the beach, and I am sure you will like Olivia. She is not hard like Irena, or brittle like Leonie. She is a girl like yourself, young and attractive, and very much in love with her husband.'

Rachel glanced Madam Sanchez's way swiftly, but her expression gave nothing away. 'And afterwards?' she ventured quietly.

Madam Sanchez lifted her shoulders and then let them fall again. 'Who knows?' she said, with a frown. 'What is certain is that you need a rest, a real rest, and that is what you will get with Marcus and Olivia.'

'Do they know I am to stay for so long?' asked Rachel, rising now, aware of that awful frustration that comes when one feels one's life is being taken out of one's hands and there is absolutely nothing one can do about it.

Madam Sanchez nodded. 'Yes, they know. Do not concern yourself on that score. Olivia was not here five years ago to pass judgements, and I doubt that Marcus would bear a grudge. You remember Marcus, I'm sure.'

Rachel nodded. Marcus was like Ramon; intelligent, gentle, and kind.... She stubbed out her cigarette and straightened. It was no good railing against a fate that so many people were mapping out for her, starting with her own father. And besides, what else could she do? Where else could she go? She didn't really want to return to London and the store so soon after her father's death, and here she was only a nuisance to her in-laws, whatever they might say. It was far better to accept the trip to Rio, let André obtain his divorce, and eventually return to London when the long summer days were beginning, and there would be fewer shadows to haunt her....

CHAPTER SIX

THE sun was beginning to slide down the sky as Rachel mounted the veranda steps and turning smiled encouragingly at Maria who lagged some few yards behind. The child's sturdy little legs were shortening their step and she looked rosy-cheeked and healthily tired. She carried a bucket in one hand and a spade in the other, and Rachel carried their two pairs of sandals. Maria clambered up the steps, and grinned triumphantly up at her aunt.

'You see,' she exclaimed. 'I told you I didn't need to be carried.'

Rachel gave her tousled hair a gentle tug, and pushed her before her into the cool tiled hall of the villa. It was refreshing to be out of the glare of the sun, but Rachel had grown quite used to its intensity during the four weeks she had been staying with Marcus and Olivia, and it no longer troubled her by its brilliance.

Maria turned as they entered the hall, and said: 'Will you give me my bath tonight, Rachel, please—oh, please!' She pulled at Rachel's hand appealingly, but just at that moment a slim attractive girl emerged from the room to their right, and said:

'Now, Maria, you've only just got home. Give Rachel a chance to sit down and have a drink. You're far too demanding! She'll be getting sick and tired of you, if you're not careful.'

Rachel smiled at her sister-in-law, and shook her head. 'No, I won't, Olivia,' she said reassuringly. 'But run along and see Tottie now, Maria. Like your mother says I want a nice relaxing cup of tea and a cigarette.'

Maria wrinkled her nose. 'Then will you bath me?'

'Most likely,' agreed Rachel, nodding, and giving the little girl's behind a sharp pat she sent her scampering off to the kitchen to find Tottie. Then she accompanied Olivia through the wide doors which led into the lounge of the villa. This was a long, low room that ran from front to back of the house, with plain white walls decorated with Brazilian carvings. The furniture was plain too, but very comfortable, and Olivia had added touches which were wholly feminine in the ribbons that looped back the heavy curtains, and the hand-embroidered cushions. It was a friendly, lived-in kind of room with toys stacked in one corner instead of stowed away in a nursery somewhere. Maria was very much a focal point in this small family, and Rachel thought that that was how it should be.

A maid had just brought a trolley of afternoon tea, and Rachel sank down thankfully, and accepted a cup from Olivia eagerly. Olivia poured her own, and then lying back in her chair, she said:

'Honestly, Rachel, I don't know how I managed before you came. You take that wretch of mine off my hands so much I'm able to do all the things I've never had time for.'

Rachel smiled. 'You must know I adore her,' she returned enthusiastically, 'and we have some good times together.'

'I can see that,' nodded Olivia, sighing. 'You wouldn't consider staying here indefinitely, I suppose?'

Rachel's cheeks coloured slightly. 'Oh, I don't know . . .' she began uncertainly.

Olivia compressed her lips. 'You don't have to decide right away,' she exclaimed. 'It's just that—well, I've discovered I'm pregnant again.'

Rachel's eyes widened. 'You are? Oh, how marvellous!'

Olivia looked doubtful. 'Do you think so? Don't you think Maria's a bit young to take to a new baby?'

'Heavens, no!' Rachel shook her head. 'She'll be four by the time it arrives. I think that's a good age. She'll be able to help you so much and she'll enjoy that. Besides, you know she's always wanting playmates.'

Olivia nodded. 'Oh, I suppose so,' she said, shrugging. 'It's just that—well, we haven't planned this baby like we planned Maria. I don't even know whether Marcus will be pleased or not.'

Rachel gave her an impatient glance. 'You haven't told him?'

'No. I—well, I've put off doing so. I suppose I shall have to sooner or later. But I shan't tell Maria until it's almost the time. Otherwise she'll grow impatient.'

'Oh, I agree with you,' said Rachel thoughtfully. Then she lit a cigarette and Olivia said quietly:

'You'd have made a marvellous mother, Rachel.'

Rachel's cheeks burned now. 'Anyone can get along

with children,' she said disclaimingly.

'No, they can't,' replied Olivia, shaking her head. 'I just can't understand——' Then she halted. 'I'm sorry. I was about to do what I promised Marcus's mother I wouldn't do—pry!'

Rachel sighed. 'It's not prying, Olivia,' she said uncomfortably. 'Naturally you're curious about me. I would be in your position. Did you know I had a miscarriage?'

Olivia nodded. 'Oh yes, I know all the facts. I just can't connect them with the woman I know.'

Rachel bit her lip. 'I'll take that as a compliment,' she commented wryly. 'I really believe I've matured somewhat since those days.'

Olivia sipped her tea, and Rachel wondered what thoughts were going through the other girl's head. From the beginning, she and Olivia had liked one another. Although Olivia's family had money and lived on the continent, the boarding schools and finishing schools she had attended had not spoiled her at all, and she was very much a home-loving girl. Marcus and Maria were her whole world, and she was not interested in any other career than that of being a good wife to her husband. But their friendship had developed in rather a limited way, for Rachel had avoided speaking about André, and Olivia had done likewise, apparently now, as Rachel had discovered, on Madam Sanchez's orders. Yet in spite of that they had become close friends, and Rachel could understand Olivia's curiosity about her situation and the uncertainties involved. Even so, she did not feel inclined to talk about her problems too much. She had successfully managed to push them to the back of her mind during her weeks here, and although she knew when she was alone in her room that nothing had really changed, she could cope with her life during the daylight hours without much difficulty, and in truth, Maria had helped enormously.

'When does Marcus get back?' asked Rachel now, changing the subject.

Olivia stretched lazily. 'Oh, the day after tomorrow,' she said, hunching her shoulders and then straightening her back. 'I usually miss him terribly when he goes away on these trips, but this time it hasn't been so bad.'

Marcus had been away for ten days. Rachel wasn't sure where he was at the moment, but the last cable they had had from him he was in New York. He had been only too glad to welcome Rachel into their home, knowing that his absences depressed his young wife when she was left alone.

Rachel smiled. 'You're only saying that,' she said patiently. 'You know you're absolutely dying to see him! You don't have to pretend indifference on my account.'

Olivia stood up. 'Oh, Rachel,' she said, shaking her head, 'I do like having you here. You will think about what I said, won't you?'

Rachel nodded. 'All right, I'll think about it,' she agreed, and getting up too, said: 'Now I'd better go and see about young Maria's bath. And you take it easy. You know you mustn't exert yourself now.'

Olivia rubbed a hand over her flat stomach. 'Oh, I'm all right,' she replied. 'It's almost seven months away yet. Just imagine, all the summer months in shapeless dresses!'

'You'll survive,' retorted Rachel unsympathetically. Then she chuckled. 'You know you're really delighted. When are you going to tell Marcus?'

Olivia lifted her shoulders. 'Oh, when he comes home, I suppose. Would you?'

Rachel felt a slight pain in the lower region of her stomach. 'Oh yes,' she said, turning away so that Olivia couldn't see her face. 'I wouldn't wait. I'm sure he'll be delighted.'

Later, in her own room, changing for dinner, Rachel sat at her dressing-table and buried her face in her hands. Somehow, Olivia's condition had brought back all the agony and misery she had hoped to forget, and there was real envy inside her for the simple happiness of Olivia's marriage. Why had she been such a fool all those years ago? If only her father had told her that André had actually followed her to London, things might have been different. But of course, he had been acting in what he thought were her best interests, and certainly from her attitude he would not have thought she wanted to see her husband. But that had all been bravado. If she had suspected André had really cared, had really forgiven her for behaving so carelessly, she would have gone to see him willingly, eagerly.... But she had thought she had killed their love and she would never have believed that André would humble himself in that way.

Getting up from her dressing-table, she walked across to the open doors that led on to a balcony. The balcony was over the veranda and her room overlooked the same sweep of Juanastra Bay as did the lounge downstairs. Below the villa, although it was now dark, there was an incline which led on to the beach, and beyond, the sweeping rollers of the Atlantic. It was a beautiful place, just outside Rio de Janeiro, with an ideal climate all the year round. There were several houses in the area, and together with some smaller cottages, they formed the village of Juanastra. It was quite a beauty spot, some of the villagers indulging in wood carving to attract the tourists. There was an old church, and some magnificent waterfalls nearby, and it was quite a busy place in the peak of the season. But where Marcus Sanchez had his house, above a private beach, it was quiet and peaceful, and until today Rachel had felt at peace there.

She supposed it was silly to let Olivia's pregnancy affect her in this way, and she *would* get over it; and she might, she just might, stay on as Olivia wanted her to do. After all, why not? It was a way of avoiding responsibilities, and right now she couldn't cope with them.

During the next couple of days Olivia prepared herself for her husband's return. She had her hair done at a salon in Rio, while Rachel took Maria shopping along the Rio Branco. The little girl was fascinated by the window displays of the huge stores, and they wandered round the departments admiring the variety of goods offered for sale. Rachel bought Maria a large drawing block and some crayons as this had become a favourite pastime of hers, and some tights and cosmetics for herself. Later they went to a coffee bar, and while Rachel had coffee Maria tackled a huge strawberry sundae topped with fresh cream and nuts. Afterwards, when they rejoined Olivia, Maria could talk of nothing else, and Olivia said good-naturedly: 'She doesn't show as

119

much excitement as this when I take her for an ice-cream. I obviously haven't the touch!'

Rachel half wished Olivia wouldn't keep saying things like that, but she meant well, and Rachel hadn't the heart to set her down. Instead, she smiled and agreed laughingly. It was late afternoon when they returned to Juanastra, and Maria shook with delight when she saw the huge car parked in front of the villa.

'Daddy's home, Daddy's home!' she screamed excitedly.

Olivia smiled apologetically at Rachel. 'Yes, I can see that,' she said. Then, self-consciously to Rachel: 'How do I look?'

Rachel studied her. 'Marvellous,' she replied, nodding. 'That hair-style suits you. I must go there myself some time.'

Olivia grimaced. 'No, you don't need a stylist,' she disclaimed. 'Yours always looks lovely, straight and thick like that. Mine has to be curled or it looks terrible.'

Olivia's hair was short and auburn, and she wore it in a curly mop. Rachel knew she knew that she was looking her best, but she needed reassurance. As they got out of the car, Rachel took Maria's hand firmly and said: 'Let Mummy say hello to Daddy first, Maria. She's excited, too, you know.'

Maria protested a little, but Olivia left them, running into the villa eagerly. Rachel and Maria followed more slowly much to Maria's annoyance, but as they reached the top of the veranda steps, Rachel let her go and she ran in to join her parents. Rachel hesitated, uncertain as to whether to go straight up to her room or to join them, when suddenly a man emerged from the lounge and stood in the hall, regarding her rather impatiently.

'André!' she said faintly, clasping the lintel of the door in an effort to retain her composure. 'Wh-what are you doing here?'

André Sanchez gave her a considering stare. 'I had some business in Rio so I flew back with Marcus,' he replied coolly. 'How are you, Rachel? You look well.'

Rachel shook her head bewilderedly. 'I—I'm fine,' she said, annoyed with herself for stammering and revealing how nervous she was. 'How—how about you?'

'I'm fine,' he replied indifferently.

'That's good.' Rachel lifted her shoulders awkwardly. 'Will you excuse me,' and brushing past him she made her way to the stairs. But Olivia's voice halted her. 'Rachel—Rachel, don't go! Come and see what Marcus has brought me—has brought *all* of us!'

Rachel compressed her lips, and then ignoring André's speculative gaze she walked into the lounge and greeted Marcus Sanchez warmly. Marcus was smaller than André, but not so lean, and his amiable face was wreathed in smiles.

'My wife tells me I have you to thank that she's not been lonely while I've been away,' he said, grinning. 'So I want you to accept this, with my thanks.'

He handed her a parcel, and awkwardly she took it. Without André's eyes upon her she would have been pleased and touched that he should have thought to bring her a gift like this, but now she wished he had not, and that she could have escaped to her bedroom to give herself time to get over the shock of seeing André. He was so cool, so indifferent, so obviously unaffected by her presence, while she shook like a rabbit in his. She was angry too. Angry that he should have deliberately come here, disturbing the peace that she had found, even if that peace was frail and capable of destruction.

With a concentrated effort, she ripped off the coloured wrapping paper round the small box in her hand. Inside she found a jewel case, and inside the jewel case was a pair of diamond pendant ear-rings. They winked in the dying rays of the sun, and Rachel looked up at Marcus with tears in her eyes. It was stupid to be emotional like this, she told herself angrily, but the ear-rings were almost identical to a pair André had once given her.

'I—I don't know what to say——' she began, shaking her head.

Marcus touched her shoulder lightly. 'It's only a gift, a bauble,' he replied gently. 'I'm glad you like them.'

André strolled across the room. 'May I see?' he queried softly, and taking Rachel's hand, he turned the box into the light. 'Hmm, very pretty,' he commented lazily. 'You have good taste, Marcus. These should be a good investment.'

Rachel closed the lid with a tiny snap. 'They're not an investment,' she said, in a curious taut voice. 'They're a gift.'

'You know what they say, darling, diamonds are a girl's best friend!' chuckled Olivia, endeavouring to lighten Rachel's mood. She had sensed that something was wrong, and she wondered whether Marcus had been aware of the foolishness of bringing his brother here at this time. Rachel sensed Olivia's discomfort and said, 'Perhaps you'll all excuse me now,' but Maria stopped her.

'Don't you want to see what I've got?' she demanded

plaintively, and at once Rachel was contrite.

'Of course I do, Maria,' she said, smiling. 'What have you got? What has Daddy brought you?'

Maria displayed her wrist. On it was a gold charm bracelet with several discs on which were carved the emblems of saints.

'Oh, that's beautiful!' exclaimed Rachel enthusiastically. 'Did you say thank you?'

'Yes, and I got this, too.' Maria produced a box in which reposed a large doll, dressed in Brazilian national costume.

'Oh, that's attractive,' said Rachel, handling the box. 'You haven't got a Brazilian doll.'

'I know. Uncle André brought it for me.'

'I see.' Rachel swallowed hard. 'That was kind of him.'

Then she moved to the door. 'I really must go and change.'

Maria frowned. 'You haven't seen the necklace that Daddy brought Mummy!' she exclaimed.

Olivia flushed. 'Rachel will see that later,' she said uneasily. 'Er—will you excuse me, too, I must go and see about your room, and dinner, André.'

André inclined his head politely, and Olivia accompanied Rachel from the room. Outside, the door closed, she said: 'I'm sorry about this, Rachel.'

Rachel managed a slight smile. 'Don't be silly, Olivia. I don't mind.' She bit her lip. 'After all, it's not as though we haven't met for some time, is it?'

Olivia sighed. 'If you say not.'

Rachel patted Olivia's arm. 'Honestly, don't worry. Just concentrate on showing your husband how pleased you are to see him home.'

Olivia was obviously relieved and she went away to the kitchen to advise Sancha that they would have a guest for dinner, while Rachel mounted the stairs to her room slowly. Her pulses were racing, and her stomach was as nervous as a butterfly. In her room, she closed the door and on impulse locked it. It wasn't that she was afraid that André might intrude but rather that Maria might come upon her crying and break the news downstairs.

She sat down on her bed and opened the jewel case again, taking out the drop ear-rings and holding them against her ears. In the mirror of her dressing-table she could see they suited her very well, and with a sigh she dropped them back into their box. Then she stripped off her clothes and went into the bathroom and turned on the shower. Under the cool water she would think more clearly.

But in fact, the shower served no useful purpose whatsoever, and she emerged, to lie on her bed, wrapped in a bathrobe, and stare at the ceiling miserably.

Why had André come here? she asked herself, again and again. He must have known what a furore it would throw her into, and after their last scene together that night on Veros, she had doubted he ever wanted to see her again. And now here he was, and she was as stupidly aware of him as a schoolgirl on her first date. Somehow, now that she had his absolute rejection, she must try and behave like an adult woman. She must behave towards him exactly as she behaved towards Marcus, if that were possible. And if that easy camaraderie was impossible, then she must maintain a kind of calm indifference, and only become involved with him as she would a stranger.

But telling herself this, in the quiet of her room was one thing. Putting such ideas into practice was quite another matter.

When the time came to dress for dinner she realised that she had forgotten to go along to Maria's room to help Tottie to get her ready for bed. Since her arrival in Rio she had always supervised Maria's evening toilette and that she had forgotten tonight proved how disturbed she was. With haste she slid off the bed and opening her wardrobe door surveyed its contents critically. Since she had been in Brazil she had bought herself several casual dresses and a couple of more elaborate gowns for evening wear, using the allowance which André had insisted on paying into an account in Rio for her. She had wanted to reject his gesture, but she realised it was impossible to exist without any money of her own. So now she drew a plain black dress from its hanger and threw it on the bed while she put on her underclothes. It did not take her long to dress and she zipped up the gown quickly and went to put the finishing touches to her hair. On impulse, she took the earrings from their case and fastened them in place. They swung against her hair, sometimes glinting through the heavy strands of chestnut, and were exactly what was needed with a dress that relied on simplicity for elegance. It was a long dress, and Rachel held up her skirts as she hurried along to Maria's bedroom.

Maria had three rooms together; a nursery-cum-dining-room, her bedroom, and her own bathroom. Rachel found Tottie in the process of trying to make Maria eat her evening meal. The little girl was dressed in pyjamas and a flowered cotton dressing-gown, and her tear-stained face bore witness to her distressed condition. When she saw Rachel, her face brightened considerably but then took on a sulky frown.

'You didn't come to give me my bath,' she accused Rachel resentfully. 'You *always* come—why didn't you come tonight?'

Rachel advanced into the room, and bent down beside Maria. 'Darling, I'm sorry,' she said cajolingly. 'Will you forgive me? I forgot the time.'

Maria looked doubtful. 'Why did you forget the time?' she asked, sniffing. 'You've got a watch.'

'I know,' Rachel sighed. 'But I'm afraid your daddy returning so excitingly like that and giving me these lovely ear-rings—see...' she flicked back her hair so that Maria could admire them, 'well, I suppose we all lost count of time.'

Maria picked at the fruit and cereal in her bowl. 'Well, all right then,' she said slowly. 'But will you promise to read me a story when I get into bed?'

Rachel glanced across at the nursery clock. It was already after seven-fifteen and she knew that Olivia would be expecting her to join them for drinks before the meal at seven-thirty. Still, she thought to herself rather desperately, this would at least give her the chance to avoid an awkward situation with André.

'All right,' she agreed. 'So hurry and finish your supper.'

Maria was obedient and quickly swallowed the rest of her meal while Tottie clicked her tongue and complained about her being spoilt. Rachel smiled at the old servant's grumbles. She was well aware that in spite of her attitude in her eyes Maria could do no wrong.

When Maria was tucked up in bed, Rachel settled down beside her and read several stories to her out of an enormous story book that had lots of colourful pictures which Maria loved to pore over. Eventually, when Maria showed no particular signs of tiring, Rachel rose to her feet.

'I must go,' she said. 'It's almost eight o'clock. Tottie, will you settle her down, please.'

Just at that moment, Olivia came into the room. She looked slim and attractive in a jade green satin gown that complemented her auburn colouring.

'So there you are, Rachel,' she exclaimed. 'Do you realise Sancha is going to serve dinner in a few minutes?'

Rachel smiled ruefully. 'I know, I'm sorry I've been so long, Olivia, but I forgot Maria's bath and I promised I'd read her a story when she was in bed.'

Olivia sighed. 'I see. Well, Maria, this is very late for you, I hope you realise that.'

Maria wrinkled her nose. 'You said you would come and say goodnight, too,' she said defensively.

'I know. I've been waiting for Rachel to come down so that I could excuse myself,' explained Olivia. 'Anyway, I'll say goodnight now, Maria, and you get yourself to sleep at once, do you hear?'

'Yes, Mummy.' Maria snuggled down, and accepted their kisses with mischievous pleasure. She was well aware of the lateness of the hour and Olivia closed her eyes in exasperation as she closed the door of Maria's bedroom.

'That little minx,' she said, shaking her head. 'She simply demands attention all the time. There's absolutely no reason why you should have to supervise her bath every evening. Particularly when we have guests like tonight.'

'Guests?' Rachel repeated, frowning.

'Of course, I haven't seen you, have I, since Marcus broke the news? André came to Rio on business, to meet this man, Alister Hemming, who is involved in one of the Sanchez mining corporations. As André was expected to dine with Hemming and his wife this evening, Marcus suggested they came and ate with us.'

'I see.'

Olivia began to descend the stairs. 'I suppose it's as well, in a way,' she commented softly. 'I mean—it will save you any embarrassment at André's presence.'

Rachel nodded. 'I suppose so,' she agreed, but she braced herself, nevertheless.

Downstairs, the two men were entertaining the Hemmings in the lounge. Lamps had been lit, and there was a friendly, intimate atmosphere of cigar smoke mingling with the aroma of alcohol. A record player issued soft music which formed a background for the buzz of conversation. André was lounging in a chair, listening intently to what Alister Hemming was saying, while he absent-mindedly swirled the liquid in his glass round and round. Marcus was leaning against the cocktail cabinet, while Mrs. Hemming was seated beside her husband, sipping some sherry.

The two men who were seated rose as Rachel and Olivia entered, and while Marcus mixed them drinks, André introduced Rachel to the Hemmings. It was, for Rachel, an awkward moment, but as usual André carried it off effortlessly, introducing her by her Christian name and thus avoiding any necessity to explain that she was his wife.

Lucy Hemming was a woman in her thirties, of medium height and build, with dark hair worn in a chignon. She was not one of those ultra-sophisticated wives some businessmen have, and Rachel suspected she would have preferred her husband to have a less demanding job. She seemed disinterested in her husband's conversation with André, and much preferred Olivia's chatter about Maria's latest antics. It transpired that Lucy had three children, two boys and a girl, all of whom attended a convent school just outside Rio. She and Olivia had a lot in common, and Rachel felt slightly *de trop*. When it came to family matters, she had nothing to offer, and instead she joined Marcus by the cocktail cabinet and accepted a cigarette from him.

'Well, Rachel?' he said, smiling as he lit her cigarette. 'You're looking particularly beautiful this evening.'

Rachel's eyes flickered. 'And that kind of talk is very good for my morale,' she commented lightly. 'Did you have a good trip?'

Marcus nodded. 'Reasonably. But New York was cold and I was glad to get back to Nassau.'

Rachel bent her head. 'Is that how you encountered André?'

'Yes. He asked me to return via New Providence, and then he decided on the spur of the moment he would come and see Hemming himself.'

'I see. His trip wasn't planned.'

'Not exactly. Originally, I was going to talk to Hemming, but I guess André decided he'd prefer to speak to him himself. Besides, André likes Rio. Surely you know that.'

Rachel coloured slightly. 'We came once,' she admitted. 'But I must admit I was surprised he came at—at this time.'

'While you're here, you mean?' asked Marcus candidly. 'Yes, so was I, frankly. But I suppose he thinks that the sooner you get used to seeing one another the better. After all, if you stay in the area at all you're bound to keep running into one another.'

'Oh, I doubt that,' replied Rachel swiftly. 'I mean—apart from the fact that I'm not likely to stay in the area—we would move in different social spheres, wouldn't we?'

Marcus frowned. 'I don't see why, Rachel. André makes you a decent allowance, doesn't he? I should imagine he would be very generous in assessing his liabilities——'

Rachel gasped. 'I don't intend to remain a liability!' she snapped, in a low voice.

Marcus heaved a sigh. 'Oh, Rachel, don't take it like that! You know I didn't mean what you're suggesting! I just meant that André doesn't have any intention of altering your standard of living——'

Suddenly Rachel became aware of someone behind her, and she swung round to find that André had joined them. His face was dark and angry, and he said in a low furious voice: 'Do you mind not discussing personal matters in front of strangers in those lucid tones!'

Rachel's colour deepened, and she turned away, leaving the brothers together just as Sancha came to announce that dinner was ready.

The long meal that followed gave Rachel a chance to recover from her annoyance, and as she was seated at the round dining table between Marcus and Alister Hemming she had no need to speak to her husband.

Alister Hemming seemed to find her fascinating, and when the meal was over it was he who escorted her back to the lounge, and sat with her on a low couch near the french doors.

Rachel enjoyed talking to him. As he was not personally involved with the Sanchez family they could discuss independent topics and as they were both interested in old books and paintings they talked quite absorbedly, so much so that Lucy Hemming disturbed them when she said, quite good-naturedly:

'Dear me, Olivia, I shall be getting quite jealous of Rachel soon, if she doesn't stop monopolising my husband.'

Rachel looked up in embarrassment to find all eyes were centred on them; Olivia and Lucy were smiling, Marcus looked amused, but André looked positively displeased.

'And if we don't continue our discussion, Hemming,' he said sharply, 'I shall wonder whether this meeting was arranged for purely social purposes!'

Alister Hemming looked embarrassed now, and rose to his feet. 'Oh, I'm sorry,' he exclaimed, running a hand through his thinning brown hair. 'But—er—Rachel—and I have a lot in common. We were just discussing the likelihood of some of these so-called classic writers of yester-year becoming famous had they lived today.'

Even to Rachel's ears it sounded a lame explanation, but unless one was intensely interested in a subject, its qualities were not always instantly apparent.

André slid his hands into the pockets of his trousers. 'Well, I suggest we go into Marcus's study,' he said coldly. 'Then we will be without the distraction of the

131

ladies.'

There was a trace of sarcasm in his voice, and Rachel wanted to say something biting to wipe that sardonic look from his face, but instead she said nothing, and the two men left the room.

After they had gone, depression settled on Rachel. Although André might create atmosphere by his coldness, at least when he was around she felt alive and aware of herself as no one else could make her.

Olivia and Lucy seated themselves together on the couch and began to talk about the problems of bringing up children in an alien environment, and as Marcus seemed quite content to lie lazily in his chair listening to the music emanating from the record player, Rachel felt her presence was unnecessary.

Trying to behave casually, she said: 'Olivia, would you think me frightfully rude if I went to bed? I—I've got a terrific headache and I think I'd like to lie down.'

Olivia was concerned. 'Oh, Rachel, are you all right?' she exclaimed, getting up and coming across to her. 'Would you like some aspirin?'

'I have some, thanks,' replied Rachel, smiling. 'Don't worry, Olivia. I'm all right. It's just a headache, that's all.'

Olivia let her go alone reluctantly, but once in her own room, Rachel heaved a sigh of relief. At least the evening was over and if André conducted his business as swiftly as was his usual way, there was a possibility that he might return to the Bahamas on the following day. Feverishly, she hoped he would. She had no intention of making a fool of herself a second time.

CHAPTER SEVEN

However, Rachel's thoughts concerning André's presence were far from accurate. On the contrary, when she came down for breakfast next morning she found André already at the breakfast table but dressed casually in navy blue shorts and shirt, thonged sandals on his bare feet. From the dampness of his hair, Rachel realised he had been swimming, and her heart lurched a little at the sight of him. He was reading a newspaper, but he put it aside when she joined him, and said:

'Olivia and Marcus aren't up yet, so I hope you don't mind my joining you for breakfast. Sancha told me you usually have it here, with Olivia.'

The table was set on the veranda, in the shade of its balconied roof, and Rachel had always enjoyed the informality of eating outside.

Shaking her head now, she said: 'You know perfectly well that as this is your bother's house, you are at liberty to eat where you choose!'

André gave her a speculative glance, noticing the shortness of the skirt of the attractive sleeveless pink cotton she was wearing, and Rachel flushed and seated herself at the table so that her legs were hidden.

'You're very brown,' he commented dryly, and then: 'Coffee?'

There was a jug beside him and she knew it would be churlish to refuse, so she nodded and he poured her some and handed her the cup. Rachel was careful to see that their hands did not touch, and then she placed the cup on the table in front of her.

Sipping the hot, aromatic beverage, she surveyed the scene before her with pleasure in spite of her disturbed thoughts. The whiteness of the sand on the beach never failed to amaze her, and it was always so beautifully clean. Breakers surged ceaselessly on to the shore-line, while in the distance some fishing boats could be seen.

André poured himself some more coffee, and then said: 'I haven't eaten yet. What do you usually have?'

Rachel compressed her lips, and turned her eyes reluctantly to his face. The lines that etched his mouth seemed more deeply engraved and she wondered if it was her imagination that made her think he looked thinner.

'Just rolls and butter,' she replied, replacing her cup in its saucer. 'I enjoy a light breakfast.'

André nodded. 'Good. I thought that was what you would say. Sancha agreed with me, so I ordered enough for two five minutes ago.'

Rachel felt her lips twitch slightly. She ought to have guessed that André would endeavour to anticipate her needs. But all she said was, 'Thank you,' and returned her gaze to the view.

But it was terribly difficult to remain composed when she was aware of his eyes upon her all the time, and she fidgeted with her hair, and smoothed her neck with one hand, trying to prevent the feeling of being appraised very thoroughly. Finally she said:

'Must you?' in a tortured voice.

André frowned. 'Must I what?' he queried coolly.

'Stare at me like that?' exclaimed Rachel. 'What idea have you now? Is it an attempt to embarrass me?

Or simply annoy me?'

André shrugged. 'I enjoy looking at you,' he replied indifferently, and Rachel's cheeks burned anew.

Sancha brought a dish of warm rolls and another containing curls of butter, and a fresh jug of steaming coffee and hot milk. Rachel helped herself to a roll, spread it liberally with butter, and took a bite. At least the food provided her with an occupation for her hands.

'Tell me,' she said suddenly, 'where are Gilroy and Sheridan? I didn't notice their obsequious presence last night.'

André's lips curved into a faint smile. 'They're staying in the village,' he replied briefly.

Rachel raised her eyebrows. 'Oh? Why?'

André sighed, and began to pare an apple. 'I knew you wouldn't care for their company,' he answered sardonically. 'Don't worry, they're within a reasonable distance.'

'I'm sure they are,' commented Rachel dryly, but she wondered why André should have taken the trouble to accommodate them elsewhere when there was plenty of room here at the villa. It couldn't be as he said, so mockingly, that he was considering her feelings. Maybe Olivia didn't like it either. In any event, it was much easier to talk without supervision, even if their conversations were barbed and barely civil at times.

André finished his breakfast, and poured himself some more coffee, then, obtaining her permission, he lit a cigar, and exhaled lazily, looking towards the horizon. Rachel was curious to know how long he intended to stay in Rio, but she could hardly come right out and ask him, could she? She sighed, and then was sorry because it attracted his attention back to her.

'Are you enjoying your stay here?' he asked, studying the tip of his cigar thoughtfully.

Rachel pushed her plate aside. 'Very much, thank you. Olivia is sweet. I like her very much, and I think she's glad of my company.'

'I told you she would be,' remarked André complacently. 'But what have you done since your arrival? Have you seen much of Rio?'

'Enough,' answered Rachel smoothly. 'I spend most of my days on the beach.'

'With Maria. I know, Olivia told me. However, I did not send you here to become Olivia's unpaid nursemaid.'

Rachel's eyes widened. 'I'm not.'

'Aren't you? Then what would you call yourself? I sent you here for a rest cure and what do I find? Frankly last evening I was amazed when Olivia explained that you usually supervised Maria's bath and got her into bed.'

'I enjoy doing it,' said Rachel stonily. 'I hope you haven't been complaining!'

André shrugged. 'If you mean have I mentioned the matter to Marcus and Olivia then I must tell you I have. We discussed it last evening after you had gone to bed.'

'You did what?' Rachel was aghast.

'You heard me, Rachel. Besides, I have other plans for you that do not involve my niece!'

Rachel shook her head impatiently. 'Honestly, André, you amaze me! You may have paid my fare here, but——'

'Please, Rachel, do not let us have another argument. You know perfectly well I am right.' He drew deeply on his cigar. 'As to my plans——'

'I'm not interested in your plans,' exclaimed Rachel. 'I don't know why you've come here, André, but I don't intend that you should humiliate me in front of your brother and his wife!'

'I do not intend to humiliate you,' he replied imperturbably, 'but I warn you, I shall not hesitate to use any authority I have to prevent you behaving like a servant.'

Rachel compressed her lips and stared down angrily at her hands. She had no doubt that André had expressed his opinion in no uncertain terms, and she felt infuriated that he still considered he had the power to direct her life. Why was he acting like this? What motive was behind it? Why should he care whether or not she looked after Maria? When she looked up again, she found him regarding her thoughtfully. Then he said:

'Do not alarm yourself, Rachel. My conversation with Marcus and Olivia was not in any way intolerant. I merely explained that I intend to spend several days in Brazil and that I mean to show you a little of the countryside around here.'

Rachel stared at him in astonishment. 'You expect me to accompany you . . .' she began incredulously.

'Is the idea so distasteful to you?' he queried politely. 'That was not my impression when last we spoke together in my mother's house.'

Rachel rose to her feet, her breast heaving. 'You *dare* to bring that up!' she cried chokingly. 'After—after what you said!'

André lay in his seat, undisturbed by her obvious

emotionalism. 'My opinion of you has not changed,' he said coldly. 'However, as I am here, and as I intend to take this break with or without your permission, I see no reason why we should not take advantage of each other's company!'

'You can't be serious!'

'Oh, but I am.' André leaned forward, resting his arms on the table. 'And you would do well not to challenge my authority!'

'Are—are—are you threatening me?' Rachel was uneasy.

André rose now. 'For heaven's sake,' he snapped impatiently. 'Why is it you can never accept a thing on its face value? You don't know Brazil well, I do. You haven't done any sightseeing, I intend to take you. Where is the harm—the threat—in that?'

Rachel linked and unlinked her fingers. 'And what if I don't want to go?' she asked unsteadily.

André lifted his shoulders and thrust his hands into the pockets of his shorts. 'This conversation bores me,' he said, ignoring her question. He glanced at the gold watch on his wrist. 'It is now a little after nine. I shall expect you to be ready to accompany me at nine-thirty, right?'

Rachel hesitated, looked as though she was going to protest, and then turned away. What was the use? So long as she was here, in his territory, she was helpless, and besides, deep inside her something primitive and urgent wanted to accept his demands and go with him no matter what his motives might be. She glanced back once and said:

'Why haven't you brought Leonie with you? Surely

she would have made a more suitable companion than me!'

André's expression was bleak. 'Leonie has gone to the States with her parents,' he replied frowningly. 'As to her company, then yes, her company would be less— shall we say—demanding than yours!'

Rachel wrinkled her nose. 'When the cat's away...' she said mockingly, and then fled before he could think up some suitable retort.

But for all her misgivings, and her discomfort at leaving Olivia to cope with Maria in her newly discovered condition, Rachel found the following days spent in André's company both mentally and physically stimulating.

From the awkward antagonism of that first morning, their relationship developed slowly, but naturally, into a restrained kind of companionship. It was impossible to maintain enmity in such idyllic surroundings, and almost without her being aware of it, Rachel began to look forward to each day with anticipation. When André set himself out to be charming she found it impossible not to respond and as the days passed she refused to look beyond the limits of his stay here. She wondered whether Leonie was aware that her proposed fiancé was in Brazil with his wife, and decided that she could not. Leonie would never have stood for that even though Rachel did not fool herself as to André's motives.

Even so, she was aware that André was deriving enjoyment from her company, and that sometimes he relaxed completely in her presence. But always something, some careless word, would recall their actual status and then André would withdraw again and become simply a charming companion.

In the beginning, they drove often into the hills, seeking the cool air of the mountains, and the delicious meals which could be had at small hostelries, but later they spent hours in Rio while André demonstrated the delights of that city to his fascinated companion. The *favellas*, the slum areas, appalled Rachel, but it was impossible to remain subdued amongst so much colour and brilliance. They bathed from Copacabana beach, Rachel had daringly bought herself a bikini of chocolate cotton, but she preferred the quieter beaches south of the city. Sometimes, lying on the beach, she would become aware of André's eyes upon her tanned body, and it was at times like these that the hazards of what she was doing struck her most forcibly. While André might be able to regard her with diluted contempt, finding aesthetic enjoyment in her company, she was always totally aware of him as a man; a man moreover, who had once shared every intimacy with her, and whose lean brown body had frequently trembled with passion in her arms.

Twice he took her to the race track, and watched with amusement as she systematically lost the sixty thousand cruzeiros he had given her to gamble with.

'Obviously you take after your father,' he remarked tolerantly, as they made their way back to the huge car-park where they had left the car. It was the first time he had mentioned her father since his arrival, and she looked up at him quickly, but there was nothing but amusement in his face.

Rachel sighed, tearing up the last race tickets she had in her hand. 'I suppose I must,' she agreed, shrugging

140

her shoulders. 'Don't you ever gamble on horses?'

André shook his head. 'One loser in the family is quite enough,' he remarked lazily, opening the door of the sleek Aston-Martin and putting her inside.

Rachel compressed her lips and watched him as he walked round the car and got in beside her. In a charcoal grey silk lounge suit, and a pale grey shirt, he looked as sleek and powerful as the automobile. Since he arrived in Brazil, he seemed to have shed some of his gravity, and while it still lurked beneath the surface, outwardly he appeared relaxed and casual. She would never have believed they could spend so many days in one another's company without creating an impossible situation. But due to André's calm, disciplined manner they were able to behave like friendly strangers. It was very rarely that she caught a glimpse of the passions he so successfully disguised, and sometimes she had an almost irresponsible urge to dispel his civilised indifference once and for all. But she always restrained herself, remembering the precariousness of her position, and trying desperately to accept that sooner or later he would return to the Bahamas and the life he led there. Sometimes she speculated on what Olivia and Marcus thought of this strange state of affairs, but it was impossible to guess, and as she and Olivia had never discussed André anyway, they didn't feel any restraint in that respect.

Now, André turned the car in the direction of Juanastra and Rachel turned sideways in her seat, resting her arm along the back of it.

'I'm surprised you don't own any racehorses,' she said conversationally.

André's long fingers curved round the steering

wheel. 'I've never found the time to study the subject,' he replied, in his usual polite manner. 'I should imagine it's an absorbing interest.'

Rachel nodded, frowning slightly. 'I suppose boats are your all-absorbing interest,' she commented.

'You could say that,' he agreed, halting at a cross-roads. The streets of Rio were thronged with people at this time of day and the traffic was thick and noisy. He looked towards her. 'Do horses interest you?'

Rachel shrugged. 'Not particularly,' she replied, shaking her head, the hair swinging against her cheek. She was wearing the diamond ear-rings Marcus had bought her, and as though compelled, André said:

'Those ear-rings: I once bought you some like that.'

'Yes, I know you did.' Rachel bit her lip. 'You'll have found them, of course. I left them behind.'

'Yes, I have your jewel case,' he said, putting the car into gear as the traffic lights changed.

They moved forward swiftly, and Rachel wondered why he should have mentioned the ear-rings suddenly. It wasn't the first time she had worn them. 'Are—are you—are you going to give them to Leonie?' she asked, the words tumbling over themselves at the finish.

André frowned. 'Of course not,' he answered, rather tersely.

'It seems a waste,' remarked Rachel quietly. 'I mean —what do you intend to do with them?'

André raised his eyebrows. 'Me? Nothing. They're not mine, Rachel, they're yours. As soon—well, as soon as the divorce is settled, I shall give them to you.'

Rachel compressed her lips trying to suppress the surge of resentment that gripped her, resentment and —*jealousy*! 'Why should you give them to me?' she asked harshly. 'As a kind of peace-offering?'

André glanced her way. 'I have no peace to make with you, Rachel,' he replied mildly. 'But if the idea offends you I won't mention it again. I'll have them valued and give you the jeweller's assessment in cash.'

Rachel clenched her teeth. 'Thank you, but that won't be necessary,' she replied tightly, and turned round in her seat so that she was not looking at him.

André made no reply to this, and she knew he would do exactly as *he* thought fit, whatever she might say. She sighed, and fumbled in her purse for cigarettes, extracting a packet and lighting one with hands that were not quite steady. Then, inhaling deeply, she tried to take an interest in her surroundings. To reach Juanastra, they passed through a narrow gorge where a waterfall tumbled continuously down the mountainside into a narrow stream that disappeared through the rocks on its way to the sea. It was a beautiful spot and it wasn't difficult to feel her tension leaving her in such surroundings. Evening was drawing in, and it would be dark soon, and the sound of the night creatures stirring mingled with the sounds of the dying day. It was not a place to wish to get lost, despite its beauty, and while the more primitive of Brazil's wildlife might exist in remoter surroundings, nevertheless, it was easy to imagine the prowling step of the mountain lion penetrating the hidden reaches of the gorge.

André spoke, breaking the uneasy silence which had fallen. 'Tell me, Rachel,' he said quietly, 'have you made any plans to return to England?'

Rachel's stomach muscles tightened. 'No,' she replied shortly.

André nodded. 'That is good,' he commented, with

satisfaction.

Rachel frowned. 'Why do you say that? Surely it's of no importance to you what I plan to do!'

'On the contrary, as Marcus pointed out when I arrived here, it would please me to know you were not moving out of my sphere.'

Rachel gave a gasp of surprise. 'Obviously, I shall return to England eventually,' she said coolly.

'Why?'

'It's my home! Besides, there's the shop...'

'The shop can be sold. I do not care for the thought of you living at the shop alone.'

Rachel gave an involuntary gesture. 'You will have to begin to accept that after the divorce, I shall no longer be under your jurisdiction!' she exclaimed.

André chewed his lower lip. 'And you know I shall not be able to accept that!' he bit out roughly, and she began to realise he was not as calm and composed as he would have her believe.

Running her tongue over her lips, she said: 'We're —we're being very intense tonight, aren't we? Perhaps we'd better change the subject!'

'No!' André was sharp. 'That is—well, I don't know whether you are aware of this or not, Rachel, but I've been here more than two weeks already and I must return to Palmerina!'

Rachel felt the blood drain out of her face and was glad of the encroaching dusk to hide her expression. 'I see,' she said, rather tautly. 'I—I suppose Leonie is due back.'

'Leonie got back three days ago!' replied André, his fingers tightening convulsively round the wheel.

'I see,' repeated Rachel, but she could think of nothing else to say. 'When—when do you leave?'

'In the morning,' replied André bleakly. 'I must confess, I shall be sorry to go. I have—enjoyed our—time together.'

Rachel's chest felt tight. 'Yes, so have I,' she managed chokily. 'At least it's given me a chance to behave like a tourist for a change.' She bit her lip to prevent it from trembling. 'I—I wish you'd told me earlier. Then I could have asked Olivia to prepare some kind of send-off party——' Her voice broke ignominiously, and with a muffled exclamation André brought the car to a halt.

'For God's sake, Rachel,' he muttered, continuing to grip the wheel tightly. 'I deliberately didn't tell you because I wanted you to enjoy our last day together.'

The compassion in his voice caught Rachel on the raw, temporarily banishing the desperation which had gripped her when he told her he was leaving. Instead, she felt anger at the pitying regret in his tone. 'Please, don't alarm yourself, André,' she retorted, rather spitefully. 'If you are afraid I'm going to make a scene, don't be. I should imagine I can leave that kind of reaction to Leonie when she discovers where you've been and what you've been doing!'

André's knuckles showed white through the skin of his hand. 'I am not in the habit of detailing my movements for any woman,' he replied coldly. 'So far as Leonie is concerned, I am away on business, and my whereabouts are my own concern.'

'Oh, I see.' Rachel managed to infuse the right amount of mockery into her tones. 'How convenient for you! Do I take it you often take time off in this underhand manner?'

André stared at her for a moment with angry, narrowed eyes, and then tearing his gaze away, he slammed the powerful car into gear and sent it hurtling off down the track. Thereafter they did not speak, until they arrived back at the villa.

During the evening that followed, Rachel was overwhelmingly conscious that in some way she had got under André's skin with her final words that afternoon. He was cold and withdrawn, not only with her but with Olivia and Marcus as well, and she realised that they had guessed, too, that something was wrong. It was a wonderful evening, a faint breeze bringing the salty tang of the sea into the lounge as they sat having coffee after dinner. But Rachel was oblivious of her surroundings and although she endeavoured to avoid André's eyes she felt them upon her and their intensity was chilling.

Marcus brought up the subject of André's departure, saying: 'Did you finalise the arrangements with Hemming?'

André inclined his head. 'By telephone, this morning,' he agreed. 'However, if anything further develops you can let me know.'

'Yes, of course,' Marcus nodded. 'Are Gilroy and Sheridan leaving with you?'

'Of course. We take off at nine-thirty.'

'You're using your own plane?'

'That's right.' André sounded bored, getting up from his seat and wandering over to the open french doors. 'I just want to say thank you for making me feel so welcome here, Olivia. I've enjoyed it, very much.'

Olivia coloured prettily. 'Why, thank you, André,' she replied, smiling. 'You must come and stay again.

Overnight accommodation is not the same as actually visiting with us.'

André turned and gave her a gentle look. 'Thank you,' he said.

Rachel moved uncomfortably. She hoped after André was gone that Olivia would not question her too closely on his reasons for being here for so long. Obviously both Marcus and Olivia had been surprised at the length of his stay, and if the days had gone fast that did not reduce their quantity. She would not have believed that sixteen days could pass so swiftly.

André's gaze flickered over her now, and then he walked decisively towards the door. 'I think, if you will excuse me, I will retire,' he said, rather broodingly. 'Goodnight.'

Marcus and Olivia answered him, but Rachel chose to ignore the moment and when she looked up again he was gone. There was a tight knot of misery in her stomach and she felt slightly sick at the knowledge that she might not see him again before he left. But in fact, she thought wearily, it might be as well if she made a point of *not* seeing him again. Their association could only cause friction now and surely he must have realised that if he came to Juanastra to punish her then he had succeeded admirably. For the first time she contemplated returning to England with real consideration. After all, sooner or later André would obtain his divorce and the next time he came to Rio he might bring Leonie with him and that would be more than Rachel could stand. She would stay for the stipulated three months, of course. It was the least she could do when Olivia and Marcus had made her so welcome, but there was no question now of her remaining until

Olivia had the baby even though the possibility had previously appealed to her. Recalling Olivia's pregnancy, she wondered whether she had told Marcus yet. During the two weeks since Marcus's return with André, Rachel had had little private conversation with her. Now Marcus began to talk about the redecoration of the lounge, and as Rachel felt no involvement she excused herself and went out on to the veranda.

She leant on the rail staring out to sea rather blindly, wondering for the hundredth time why André had chosen to come to Brazil and spend these two weeks with her. That he had enjoyed her company, she had no doubt, but there seemed no point in it all. Unless...

Her pulses raced at the thought that perhaps André still found himself attracted to her in spite of himself. It was possible; physically she did attract him, but at no time during his stay had he made any attempt to touch her and even this afternoon when she had aroused him so badly, he had refrained from wreaking any revenge upon her. It was a strange and disturbing situation. André was completely in control of himself and she was foolish to imagine he felt anything more than contempt for her. Maybe some innate sense of cruelty had compelled him to come here and destroy what little peace of mind she had achieved.

She compressed her lips and breathed deeply. Either way, it didn't matter now what his motives had been. He was leaving in the morning and she might never see him again. Indeed, if she left for England within the next couple of months there was absolutely no reason why she should ever see him again.

Later, when she had composed herself, she returned

to the lounge, but she found Marcus was alone. 'Olivia has gone to bed,' he said apologetically. 'She's been rather off colour all day, and she hoped you wouldn't mind.'

Rachel managed a faint smile. 'Of course not,' she exclaimed sympathetically. 'Is she all right? Is there anything I can do?'

'Oh no, I don't think so,' Marcus shook his head. 'She's rather tired, that's all. Been overdoing it, I suppose. She told you about the baby, I understand.'

Rachel nodded, glad that Olivia had told Marcus. 'Yes,' she nodded. 'Were you pleased?'

Marcus shrugged. 'I guess so. We'll have to have a permanent nanny now, though. Olivia just can't cope.' He frowned. 'I believe she asked you to stay on. If you agreed to do so, I should be very grateful, but I should insist on putting you on a monthly salary....'

Rachel sighed. 'I'm sorry, Marcus, but it's out of the question,' she said regretfully.

Marcus lifted his hands. 'But why? Your status here wouldn't change. You'd still be a member of the family, but naturally I couldn't let you help without——'

'It's not that, Marcus, honestly,' exclaimed Rachel, shaking her head. 'I'm not proud. I'd accept a salary, although I doubt whether I would need it while André is paying me such an enormous allowance. No, it's not that—it's just—well, I really think I will eventually return to London.'

Marcus sighed heavily. 'Well, you know best about that, of course, but don't decide right now. Keep it in your mind! There's no hurry. It's seven months before Olivia has the baby.'

Rachel smiled. 'All right,' she agreed quietly. 'I'll keep it in mind, and thank you, Marcus.'

Marcus shook his head. 'It's I who should be thanking you,' he maintained. 'Since you came you've helped Olivia a lot. She's really taken to you, you know.'

Rachel bit her lip. 'And I like her, Marcus, really I do. It's just—well—things!'

Marcus bent his head. 'André.'

'I suppose so.' Rachel twisted her hands awkwardly.

'I see.' Marcus turned away. 'Well, if you change your mind. . . .'

Rachel nodded and then made her way across the room to the door. 'I—I think I'll go to bed, too,' she said self-consciously. 'Goodnight, Marcus.'

Marcus looked up from lighting a cigar. 'Goodnight, Rachel,' he said gently.

Rachel made her way upstairs feeling slightly tearful. Marcus and Olivia had been so kind. They had not condemned her for her actions five years ago, even though they did not know the whole truth of that affair, and they had made her feel really as one of the family. She would be sorry to leave them, and there was no doubt that she would miss Maria whom she had sadly neglected since André arrived.

Reaching her room, she entered and did not immediately switch on the light, walking over to her balcony to lean on the rail dejectedly. But she became conscious of other sounds in the room, and with a feeling akin to panic she moved to the bed and switched on the bedside light, flooding the room with its mellow glow.

Then she gasped, pressing a hand to her throat nervously. André was seated in the armchair at the foot of her bed. He had discarded his dinner jacket, and tie, and was wearing only the silk evening shirt and dark trousers. He had unbuttoned the shirt as though he was too warm, and from the slightly rumpled state of his hair he seemed to have been running his hands through it pretty frequently.

As she endeavoured to recover from the shock of seeing him there, she said: 'What—what do you want?'

André did not rise but continued to regard her solemnly. 'I wanted to talk to you,' he said tautly, 'and as it was impossible downstairs I decided to wait for you here.'

'I see.' Rachel pulled her ear-rings from her ears and smoothed her hair in a nervous way. 'What do you want to talk to me about?' She was aware of the jerky breathiness of her voice and wished she could sound cool and indifferent, but that was impossible.

André was sitting with one long leg draped over the arm of the chair and he looked completely at his ease. 'When your three months here are up, what do you plan to do?' he asked shortly.

Rachel lifted her shoulders. 'I—I haven't decided yet,' she replied unevenly. 'Besides, it's nothing to do with you, and I don't think you have the right to ask me.' She straightened her back rather stiffly.

André swung his leg to the ground and stood up. 'Rights,' he commented tersely, 'what are rights? Do you know? I doubt it.'

Rachel swallowed hard. 'This is my bedroom, and I think I have the right to demand that you leave it,' she exclaimed, and André uttered an exclamation.

'Keep your voice down,' he commanded angrily. 'Or

do you want the whole household to hear our conversation?'

'There is to be no conversation,' retorted Rachel, in a low voice. 'Will you please leave?'

André turned away, thrusting his hands into the pockets of his trousers. 'Rachel,' he said, in a low appealing voice, 'try and understand my position. For seven years I have been responsible for you, and I am now aware that apart from me you are alone in the world, at least so far as relatives are concerned. I must know what you intend to do so that I may help you if you need help, or offer advice if advice is needed. You know that money is no object. If there is anything you want, anything you need——'

The faint strains of some music Marcus was playing downstairs drifted through the balcony doors making a mockery of their argument. It was such a beautiful night, the stars brilliant in a sky of dark blue velvet. There were flowers outside, the perfumes of which wove their own spell of magic, and Rachel wondered how anyone could remain immune to such an onslaught of enchantment. It was a night of enchantment, not a night for arguments or angry words. It was a night made for love and for lovers, and the sweet triumphant satisfaction of surrender. How could André be unaware of such things? She knew an overwhelming desire to move closer to him, to slide her arms around him, and make him aware of her as a woman, and not as some annoying liability.

Hardly aware that she spoke, she murmured: 'André!' achingly, and something in her voice made him turn to look at her.

His eyes slid over her compulsively appraising the

simple white gown edged with red braid which she had bought several weeks ago in Rio. Its plain lines drew attention to the creamy tan of her skin; the low neckline revealed the rounded swell of her breasts, while its ankle length gave her a bridelike elegance. With deliberate movements, she pulled the white band from her hair so that it swung silkily against her cheeks, thick and smooth.

André shook his head. 'No,' he groaned suddenly. '*No!*'

Rachel watched him with her slanted green eyes for a moment, and then she said: 'I really think you must go, André. This—this isn't the time, or the place, to conduct the kind of conversation you seem to want. . . .'

André took a step towards her compulsively, clenching his fists. 'You have no conception of what I want!' he muttered savagely.

Rachel bent her head. 'Please, André,' she began, realising the iron self-control he possessed was slipping badly, 'there's nothing more to be said.'

'Damn you, isn't there?' he swore violently. 'Rachel, don't try me too far!'

Rachel lifted her head and stared at him. 'I suggest you leave one of your henchmen behind,' she said bitterly. 'Then he can report to you on my movements!' She turned away abruptly. 'Oh, go—please go! I can't stand much more of this!'

André moved and she felt the heat of his body close behind her. One hand slid across the bare skin of her shoulder and up her neck to her ear, caressing it almost compulsively. 'Do you think I am so unfeeling?' he demanded in a tortured voice. 'Do you imagine that being here alone with you doesn't put thoughts into

153

my head?' His other hand slid over her waist and Rachel began to find it difficult to get her breath.

'What—what thoughts?' she faltered, running her tongue over lips that were suddenly dry.

'Thoughts of making love to you,' he murmured huskily, catching the tip of her ear between his teeth and biting gently. 'This is really the whole trouble, isn't it?' he groaned, breathing swiftly and unsteadily. 'I want you, Rachel, just like you said, and dear God, I think I've got to take you!'

Rachel twisted round in his arms, her eyes wide. 'André ...' she whispered questioningly.

'Yes,' he said roughly, pressing her body close against his. 'Yes, Rachel.' His mouth caressed her neck, and as it sought her mouth, he murmured, 'Oh, God, just let me love you ...' and then he kissed her with demanding intensity.

Rachel was unable to resist the inevitable. His touch sent the blood singing in her ears and she wound her arms round his neck and trembled as his hands caressed her body. Presently, he picked her up bodily into his arms, and carried her to the bed, sliding down beside her and extinguishing the light before his mouth covered hers. There was no thought of whether it was right or wrong, just the overpowering urgency of their need for one another....

CHAPTER EIGHT

RACHEL was awakened by someone bouncing mercilessly on the end of the bed, and she couldn't imagine for a moment who it could be. She felt an unusual desire to remain where she was and she opened her eyes reluctantly. But even as she recognised Maria's mischievous little face peeping at her from the bottom of the bed realisation of the previous night's events came to her, and she rolled swiftly over to look at the other side of the bed. Apart from the imprint of a head on the pillows there was no evidence of André's occupation, and a mixture of relief and despair swept through her.

Maria slid off the bed and came along to her wrinkling her nose. 'Mummy said I might wake you up,' she said. 'It's very late!'

Rachel pressed a hand to her temples, and struggled into a sitting position, holding the silk sheets close about her body. Blinking, she tried to focus on the travelling clock on the bedside table, and her eyes widened when she saw the time. It was after ten-thirty, and she fell back on her pillows disbelievingly. Had she really slept so long? And where was André now? Had he left as planned, or was he waiting for her downstairs? Even before she formulated the question, she knew the answer. He was a man of his word.

Looking at Maria through glazed eyes, she said: 'Er—Uncle André has gone?' as casually as she could.

Maria frowned. 'Oh yes, hours ago,' she nodded. 'Why? Did you want to say goodbye?'

Rachel swallowed hard, and bit her lips. 'Oh—oh no,' she denied, swiftly. 'Er—I must have overslept. Off you go now, Maria, and I'll get dressed. Tell Mummy I'm sorry to be so late.'

Maria frowned. 'Will you really get up?' she asked suspiciously. 'I mean—now that Uncle André's gone you won't be so busy, will you?'

Rachel managed a faint smile. 'No, I won't be so busy,' she reassured her. 'Now off you go! I must get dressed.'

Maria went out closing the door behind her, and Rachel waited until the child's footsteps died away down the corridor before turning her head and burying it in the pillow where André's head had rested....

But of course, she had to get up, and eventually she dried her eyes and slid out of bed, noticing with pained eyes how the garments she had worn the night before were strewn carelessly about the floor. In the bathroom she took a long, refreshing shower and then dressed in a tunic of tangerine cotton. All the while she attended to her toilette, she tried unsuccessfully not to think about the events of the night before and their implications for her. But it was impossible to ignore the lethargy of her limbs and the painful yet delicious recollection of André's lovemaking. At least it had proved that she still attracted him, but that was all. At no time had he led her to believe that he needed her in any other capacity. And he had continued with his plans to leave this morning, almost as though nothing had happened of any consequence.

Her hand trembled as she applied some lipstick. She was the fool as usual. She had allowed him to make love to her knowing that to him it could mean nothing but a sexual experience.

And why had she allowed it to happen? How had he succeeded? Had he taken advantage of her? *No!* She had been a willing victim to his charm, to the enchantment of the night. And it had been enchanted, of that there was no doubt.

She compressed her lips and stared blindly at her reflection. Somehow she had to put last night out of her mind, but how she was to achieve such a thing she had no idea.

Downstairs, Olivia was in the lounge taking morning coffee and she smiled welcomingly when she saw Rachel.

'So there you are!' she exclaimed. 'I had to let Maria come up to you. She's been agitating to see you since about eight-fifteen. You must have been tired.'

Rachel coloured delicately. 'Yes,' she said non-committally. 'How—how are you this morning? Marcus told me you weren't too well last evening.'

Olivia shrugged. 'Oh, you know,' she said lightly. 'Just the usual nausea that accompanies my condition. How anyone can ever call it an interesting condition, I'll never know. So far as I am concerned, it's very uninteresting!'

Rachel helped herself to some coffee and lit a cigarette, refusing Olivia's offer of obtaining breakfast for her. 'I'm not hungry,' she explained smilingly. 'Besides, it's too near lunch time.'

Olivia looked down at the sewing in her lap. She was smocking a dress for Maria, her small, neat stitches a delight to the eye. 'Tell me,' she said quietly, 'did you say goodbye to André?'

Rachel drew on her cigarette. 'I guess so,' she replied awkwardly. 'We—I suppose you could say we said our goodbyes yesterday.'

'Oh, I see.' Olivia nodded. 'I thought he seemed rather annoyed about something last night, didn't you?' She sighed. 'This morning he left without hardly

157

saying a word, and he didn't want any breakfast either. Did you have a row or something?' Then she bit her lip. 'Oh, I'm sorry, I'm doing exactly what Marcus said I mustn't do—being inquisitive!'

Rachel shook her head. 'It's all right, Olivia,' she said. 'And no—we didn't have a row exactly, although I said some pretty hateful things to him!'

'I wonder why he stayed so long?' Olivia mused curiously. 'I mean—he didn't have to take you out with him, did he? If you ask me, I think he still feels responsible for you.'

Rachel gave a short mirthless laugh. 'Yes,' she said unsteadily, 'I suppose you could say he feels responsible for me. It's part of the Sanchez family tradition, didn't you know?' She clenched her fists in her lap. 'Even though André has every intention of marrying Leonie, he still can't accept that I expect real freedom. He seems to imagine himself some kind of eastern potentate who can take more than one wife and therefore continue to control both their destinies.' Her voice was harsh at the end, and Olivia uttered an exclamation.

'But, Rachel,' she cried, 'don't you think you're being a little irresponsible yourself? I mean'—she hastened on—'I mean obviously you need André's help and guidance now that your father is dead. You have no one else, no other relatives. Why shouldn't he help you——'

'Everyone seems to imagine I'm incapable of looking after myself,' Rachel exclaimed impatiently. 'Your life may have been cushioned, Olivia, but before I married André I had been used to looking after my father, too. And during the past five years, I guess I've grown accustomed to being alone.'

Olivia shrugged her shoulders. 'All right, Rachel,' she said quietly, 'don't get angry with me! I only want what's best for you. I've grown very fond of you since you've been staying here, but I just wish you'd put all ideas of returning to England out of your mind and remain here with us.'

Rachel gave a rueful gesture. 'I'm sorry, Olivia,' she said apologetically. 'It's just that—well, I suppose I'm on edge. I'll be all right in a day or two.'

Olivia leaned forward and pressed her arm understandingly. 'Maria has gone down to the beach with Tottie,' she said. 'Why don't you go and get your swim suit and join them? I think you need uncomplicated, unsophisticated company,' she smiled.

'Perhaps I do at that,' agreed Rachel, getting to her feet. 'And thank you, Olivia, for not asking too many questions. One day I'll try and explain everything that's happened, but right now I can't.'

Later in the morning, lying on the sands with Maria, Rachel wondered how long it would take for her to recover from the impact of André's visit. At no time during their tempestuous relationship of five years ago had she felt such a devastating sense of despair, and she realised that her feelings for André had matured as she had matured. It would be infinitely more difficult to assume a cloak of normality now than it was then. For one thing she was five years older, and for another, no matter how she might protest that she was capable of taking care of herself, she was completely alone, and that was quite a devastating realisation.

But the human body has incredible powers of recovery, and time, though it may not actually heal a wound, can put a protective shield over it so that the pain is not so acute. Rachel discovered this during the weeks following André's return to Palmerina. To begin with it was terribly hard to feel anything but self-pity and despair, but gradually her natural resilience asserted itself and she began to accept that life must go on. Marcus's departure on a prolonged trip to Europe made her realise how selfish she was being in only thinking of her own problems, and after he had gone she tried to make Olivia's life more bearable. Olivia was not having an easy pregnancy, and most days she was violently sick or developed terrible headaches. André had taught Rachel to drive when they were first married, so now Rachel chauffeured Olivia's convertible and took her out along with Maria, away from the stifling atmosphere of the villa. Olivia enjoyed these outings, and they brought colour to her otherwise pale cheeks.

The weeks slipped away and Rachel began to realise that soon her three months' stay would be over. She knew Olivia was dreading her leaving, but somehow she felt she must.

One afternoon, about a month after André's departure, Rachel drove Olivia and Maria to a place in the mountains for an early evening meal. The village sported an excellent restaurant as well as having the advantage of overlooking a mountain lake. It was very peaceful there in the early evening and it wasn't their first visit. But today Rachel herself felt moody and out of sorts, and half-wished she had not volunteered to drive so far. However, Olivia and Maria were in high spirits. Marcus was due to return in a couple of days, and they chattered about nothing else.

They ate an iced consommé, followed by steaks and

salad, and finished with salted biscuits and spicy Brazilian cheese, but all Rachel could manage was a little of the salad. Her stomach was behaving in a most objectionable way, and she could only assume it was something she had eaten earlier in the day.

They drove home in the darkness, the headlights picking out the narrow, winding mountain road. Rachel wondered whether she should ask Olivia to drive, but decided against it. She didn't want to worry her when she seemed to be enjoying herself so much, but as they neared the outskirts of Juanastra, Rachel was forced to stop the car, and hastily opening the door she ran into the bushes at the side of the road, and vomited violently. Afterwards she lay against a tree for a moment while the world swam round her in a hazy, nauseating fashion.

Olivia came hurrying across to her, looking anxious. 'Rachel!' she exclaimed, frowning. 'Whatever is the matter?'

Rachel managed a faint smile. 'It's nothing, Olivia. I'm sorry to be such a nuisance. It must be something I've eaten. I just felt terribly sick suddenly.'

Olivia studied her pale face in the moonlight and shook her head. 'Come on back to the car,' she urged gently. 'We're almost home, and I'll drive from here.'

'Oh, that's not necessary,' exclaimed Rachel apologetically. 'I'll be okay....'

'Of course you will,' said Olivia soothingly, leading her back to the car. 'But I'll drive just the same. Look, slide into my seat.'

Rachel did as she was told, and Olivia climbed in beside her, looking at her ruefully, a smile appearing mischievously as she saw Rachel was recovering her colour. 'If no one knew which of us was pregnant, they'd imagine it was you, Rachel,' she joked.

Luckily for Rachel, Olivia was intent on starting the car and answering Maria's troubled questions, and she did not notice the tense white expression on her companion's face. Rachel closed her eyes for a moment, pushing back her hair with a trembling hand. Oh God, she thought agonisingly, why didn't I think of that?

She ran a hand over her damp forehead and blinked rapidly. It couldn't be true, she tried to tell herself severely. Just because Olivia was pregnant she naturally associated everything with her condition. And in any case she had not been serious.

But as Rachel sat there, unaware of everything but the frightening absorption of her thoughts, a compelling kind of instinct warned her it was not an idea that should be dismissed lightly. She had been so engrossed with her own misery she had not considered the normal functions of her body and now that she did she began to realise that this was something she should have suspected days ago.

Perspiration trickled down her spine, and the dizziness returned in full force, brought on as much by sheer panic as by the motion of the vehicle. What a ghastly situation to find herself in. And what could she do now?

The car turned between the gates of the villa and Olivia drew up at the foot of the veranda steps.

'You go in and take a shower, Rachel,' she said gently, urging her out of the car. 'It must be the heat, catching up with you at last. Most people are affected by it some time.'

Rachel nodded gratefully, unable to speak or even

think coherently, but she did as Olivia suggested and took a shower, glad of the refreshing stream of cool water against her hot skin. Afterwards, she deliberately examined her slim body in the tall mirrors on the bathroom wall. But in spite of her fears, there were no outward physical signs that anything momentous had happened, and she wondered if she could be mistaken. Had she let Olivia's casual words assume a greater significance than they possessed?

She shook her head in bewilderment and went to dress. She would just have to wait and see. She could hardly take her problems to the Sanchez family doctor without causing a great deal of curiosity. But if she was pregnant, she ought to consider what she was going to do about it, she thought rather frantically. Was she going to tell André, for example?

The answer to that was quite definite—*no*! She had no intention of creating a situation he would be forced to honour knowing his sense of family responsibility. So then she was left with two alternatives: either she made some enquiries into the possibility of obtaining an abortion when she got back to England, or she had the child and brought it up herself.

As these alternatives ran through her mind she knew with certainty what she would do. On no account could she destroy the child of their love so deliberately. It was no use quibbling that André's involvement had been physical rather than spiritual. This child that might now be forming in her womb was the living, breathing result of their union and she wanted it— there was no possible doubt about that, however difficult she might find the responsibilities in later years.

The decision made, all that was left was for her to

allay any suspicions Olivia might formulate during the couple of weeks of her stay that was left. But of course Olivia had no reason to suspect anything and she accepted Rachel's explanation that she must have eaten something that disagreed with her to cause her to feel so ill.

During the next ten days Rachel was forced to realise that she was indeed pregnant. She had all the usual symptoms: early morning nausea, acute tiredness, and a dislike for any kind of narcotics. She cut her smoking down to a minimum and only drank coffee when she was forced to do so. Marcus returned from his European tour, alone this time, and Maria deserted Rachel to spend her time with her beloved daddy. Olivia continually brought up the question of Rachel staying on in Brazil, but when it became apparent that she was determined to leave Olivia helped her to make her travel arrangements. Marcus had added his own inducements to his wife's, and Rachel knew he was concerned about her being left alone when he went on his next trip. Therefore it was really no surprise when towards the end of the second week Marcus telephoned his mother asking her whether she couldn't possibly come and stay for a few weeks. Madam Sanchez however was just recovering from a severe cold and was not really fit to travel.

Olivia was in the room while Marcus made his call, showing Rachel how to embroider motifs on to pillowslips, and she looked up when she realised the trend of the conversation. 'It doesn't matter!' she exclaimed, rather tiredly. 'Marcus, I'll be perfectly all right.'

Marcus shook his head at her and continued to talk to his mother, and when he finally replaced the receiver he seemed well pleased. 'Irena is coming,' he said firmly. 'She's arriving tomorrow. Now I know you'll be fine.'

Olivia's eyes flickered to Rachel. 'I see,' she said, her tone conveying very clearly that such a compromise was not particularly to her liking.

Marcus frowned. 'What's wrong now?' he asked impatiently. 'Irena is my sister. Surely she will be a suitable substitute for Rachel!' He looked apologetically at his sister-in-law. 'Rachel knows I don't mean any harm by that. We would prefer her to stay, she knows that, but as she can't, Irena will take her place.' He sighed. 'Later, perhaps, you could go and stay on Veros for a while, Olivia.'

Olivia licked her lips. 'All right, Marcus, don't alarm yourself! If my enthusiasm about Irena coming seems slightly strained, it's merely because I've grown used to Rachel, and she's good with Maria. Irena isn't exactly anybody's idea of the perfect nanny!'

Marcus uttered an exclamation and marched out of the room, and Olivia compressed her lips resignedly. 'Oh, heavens, now he's annoyed,' she said, sighing. 'Honestly, Rachel, I don't mean to be unkind, but Irena and I have never been what you might call friends.'

Rachel, with her knowledge of Irena, dared make no comment. It would not be fair to criticise Irena and alienate Olivia's relationship with her still further. So she smiled sympathetically, and changed the subject.

Irena arrived late the following afternoon. Rachel was glad her stay had only another full day remaining. Somehow Irena's eyes stripped away her defences, and Rachel almost felt that she might immediately suspect

165

that something was wrong.

But luckily Marcus was around to ease the situation, and as Irena had arrived to help Olivia, she put herself out to make herself useful, ignoring Rachel whenever possible, and making her feel useless and unwanted.

Still, Rachel argued with herself, that was how she wanted it to be. She didn't want to feel guilty about leaving Olivia alone, and no matter how poor a companion Irena might be she would be there to help if any help was needed.

The night before Rachel was due to leave, Olivia gave a small dinner party. It was quite a success, and Rachel felt a sense of gratitude towards Olivia and Marcus for making her so welcome in their home. There was no doubt that she would miss them and the beauty of Juanastra Bay. Maria had been subdued, too, when Rachel saw her into bed, for the little girl cared little for her Aunt Irena.

Olivia retired directly the party was over. She was still rather unwell, and Rachel felt quite anxious about her. She determined to write frequently to her once she got back to England, and maybe some day she would be able to come back and see them.

Rachel helped Sancha to clear away the debris after the guests had departed and Marcus said goodnight, and it wasn't until Rachel went back into the lounge to see whether she had missed any glasses that she found Irena waiting for her. At first, she thought their meeting was accidental, but Irena walked past her and closed the door, saying: 'I want to talk to you, Rachel,' in a cold restrained tone.

Rachel compressed her lips. She had no desire to talk to Irena and had hoped she was going to escape such a scene, but it was obvious that Irena had something to say and she intended to say it with or without Rachel's permission.

Irena lit a cigarette before beginning, and Rachel contemplated ignoring her altogether and leaving the room, but she knew that would make her appear a moral coward, and while she did not like Irena, she certainly did not fear anything she might say to her.

'Please, Irena,' she said now, 'tell me what it is you have to say, and then let me go to bed. I'm very tired, and I have to be up early tomorrow morning.'

Irena exhaled and regarded her through a veil of tobacco smoke. 'Don't alarm yourself, Rachel, what I have to say won't take long.' She walked slowly across to the french doors which still stood wide to the night air. 'Did you know that André has applied to the courts for his divorce? If everything goes according to plan, he and Leonie will be married before the end of the year.'

A knife turned in Rachel's stomach. 'Is that all you have to tell me?' she asked tautly.

Irena shook her head. 'That's part of it, Rachel,' she replied, with a mocking smile. 'This is the rest.' She opened her evening bag and extracted a piece of paper. 'André asked me to give you this. He said you would know what it was for.'

Rachel frowned, taking the slip of paper and opening it with trembling fingers. It was a cheque for five thousand pounds. She stared at it disbelievingly, and then looked up uncomprehendingly at Irena. Swallowing hard, she said faintly: 'I don't understand; what is this?'

Irena gave her a speculative glance, noting her pale

cheeks and shaken appearance. 'I understood you would know what André meant,' she said chillingly. 'Surely you understand why he sent it?'

Rachel stared again at the cheque. It was André's handwriting all right, and it was dated only three days ago; the day Irena left for Brazil. 'He—he gave you this!' she murmured, almost inaudibly, her emotions churning nauseously.

'Of course.' Irena shrugged her narrow shoulders. 'Honestly, Rachel, don't look so shook up! It's only money!'

Rachel felt mortified. That André should send her money was bad enough; that he should send it with Irena was doubly humiliating.

With an overwhelming feeling of faintness enveloping her, Rachel knew she had to get out of the room before she disgraced herself in front of her sister-in-law. But before she left she tore the cheque into a dozen tiny pieces, scattering them in Irena's face with childish retaliation.

'You—you can tell your brother I don't want his filthy money!' she cried, groping her way to the door. 'I never did!' and with that she wrenched open the door and went out into the cool hall.

She stood for a moment, waiting for the dizziness to recede, and then made her way unsteadily to her bedroom. She would never have believed André could be so cruel, so unfeeling, or that he could have thought to humiliate her like that in front of Irena. What had he told his family about their relationship that Irena should speak with such confidence about the reasons for him offering her money? How could he have betrayed her like that, at a time when she was actually

168

bearing his child? It was horrible, *unthinkable*! What did it matter that he knew nothing about the baby, he surely could not have lost all respect for her so swiftly! Or had she been right in her assumption that his reasons for coming to Brazil had been ones of revenge, and that this final humiliation had been his winning card...?

CHAPTER NINE

It took Rachel several weeks to accustom herself to life in London again. There was so much to do, so many things to arrange, and over and above all the pain she felt when she visited her father's grave was the agony of self-recrimination she felt when she recalled the way André had treated her.

It was so strange to live again in the flat above the shop but alone now in a world grown alien by her father's absence. Mrs. Verity, who kept the adjoining newsagents, seemed to be the only person she really knew, for since her marriage to André she had not made many friends. People did come to see her, old friends of her father's, but there was no one close enough for her to share any confidences, and she seemed to shrink within a shell so that her manner did not encourage overtures from outsiders.

The shop needed a thorough cleaning, and she was grateful when Mrs. Verity's daughter, Hannah, offered to give her a hand. Between them they managed to shift everything, sweeping and whitewashing so that the old place began to smell fresh again. Hannah's boyfriend, John Adamson, came to help them and he moved all the heavier items, for which Rachel felt an immense sense of relief. She knew that too much exertion might harm the baby.

During the weeks of the cleaning, she got to know Hannah and John quite well, and they managed to penetrate the shield of aloofness that she had caught about her. She knew that sooner or later she would have to tell them of her condition, for although she remained quite healthy, it would inevitably begin to show.

When the shop was finished, she went to see the solicitor again; she had seen him first soon after her arrival back in England, and she asked his advice about the advisability of selling. Mr. Cropper was quite a young man, and he regarded Rachel rather speculatively.

'You want to sell?' he enquired.

Rachel hesitated. 'I'm not sure,' she admitted. 'It's just that—well, I wondered whether it might be a good idea.'

Mr. Cropper shrugged. 'It rather depends what you intend to do, doesn't it, Rachel,' he said thoughtfully. 'I mean—your father explained to me that you might be going to live in the Bahamas, but now that you're back do you intend to stay?'

Rachel bit her lip. 'Oh yes, I intend to stay,' she answered.

Mr. Cropper frowned. 'Then in that case, if, and I say if, you sell the shop, what do you intend to do—where do you intend to live? And have you another income?'

'If I sell the shop, I expect I shall be able to find a flat somewhere,' she replied. 'Then—later—I could get a job. I'm a qualified librarian.'

Mr. Cropper studied her. 'But surely, Rachel, if you do sell the shop, you realise you may find the rents currently being charged in the metropolitan area rather exorbitant for your means.' He sighed. 'Come now, Rachel, tell me honestly, why do you want to sell a business that could conceivably provide you with a comfortable living? Your father let everything slide. It's up to you to take it in hand and make a success of it!'

Rachel bent her head. 'I'm afraid the shop might be too much for me,' she said slowly.

'Too much for you!' echoed Mr. Cropper incredulously. 'A young woman of your age could take a business like that in her stride!'

Rachel looked at him steadily. 'I'm pregnant, Mr. Cropper,' she said quietly.

Harold Cropper was taken aback. His rather florid features took on a purplish tinge and he looked absolutely embarrassed. 'I—I see,' he said, obviously astounded by this revelation. 'I'm sorry, Rachel, I had no idea. . . .'

'Why should you have?' asked Rachel dryly. 'But as I am, and as you now know, what do you suggest I do?'

'Tell me,' he said, recovering slightly and wiping his forehead with a handkerchief. 'Your husband—he is still your husband, isn't he?' and at her nod, he continued: 'Does he know about—well, this other man?'

Rachel compressed her lips. 'There is no other man, Mr. Cropper,' she said distinctly.

'You mean. . . .'

'Yes. This is my husband's child.'

'Then for God's sake, what is he doing letting you

come back here alone to attempt to start up an old business——'

'He doesn't know.'

'He doesn't know?'

'No. And I don't intend to tell him. So can we go on. . . .'

'Just a minute!' Mr. Cropper swallowed hard. 'Rachel, you can't just come in here with a story like this and expect me to give you a decision just out of my head. I need time to think—to assimilate what you've told me. For heaven's sake, why haven't you told him?'

'My husband is in the process of obtaining a divorce,' replied Rachel calmly.

Mr. Cropper shook his head. 'Then how——' he began, and then halted. 'I'm sorry, Rachel, if I sound old-fashioned, but I was a friend of your father's, and quite honestly I think you're making a terrible mistake allowing your husband to obtain his divorce without telling him of your condition. Good heavens, it's his child, too.'

'André has no rights where this child is concerned,' said Rachel bitterly. 'He paid for it with a cheque for five thousand pounds.'

'Five thousand pounds!' Mr. Cropper was obviously out of his depth. 'You have the cheque?'

'No. I tore it up.'

Mr. Cropper could not have looked more perplexed, but manfully he refrained from making any further observations even though it was obvious that he would have loved to continue discussing what had occurred. Eventually he said:

'I think, as I said, Rachel, I need time to think this over; will you come back and see me in—say—two or three days, and I'll try and have an answer for you?'

Rachel nodded. 'All right.' Then a thought struck her. 'You don't have it in mind to attempt to tell my husband what I've told you, do you?' she asked suspiciously.

Mr. Cropper looked put out. 'Of course not. My clients' affairs are confidential, as you know,' he exclaimed.

Rachel allowed herself a smile as she rode back to Chelsea in the bus. Mr. Cropper was such a transparent person, and quite obviously he found it difficult to accept her explanations. But she trusted him implicitly, and he had been a good and loyal friend to her father despite the fact that he was years younger.

Hannah Verity came round soon after Rachel's return, and she found Rachel stretched out on the couch in the small living-room of the flat. She was a nice girl, round and comely, with long straight fair hair and blue eyes.

'Hey!' she exclaimed, when she saw Rachel. 'You look pale, Rachel. Are you all right?'

Rachel smiled. 'I just feel a bit tired, that's all,' she admitted. 'Would you make me a cup of tea, Hannah? I just got back about a quarter of an hour ago, and I'm dying for one, but I hadn't the energy.'

'Sure thing.' Hannah went into the tiny kitchen and busied herself putting on the kettle and setting out the cups. Then she came back to the door of the living-room. 'Would you like me to go round for Mam?' she asked anxiously.

Rachel smiled again. 'Oh no, Hannah, I'll be okay.' Then she sighed. 'Oh, you've got to know sooner or later, anyway, I'm going to have a baby.'

Hannah's eyes widened miraculously. 'You're pregnant!' she exclaimed. 'Oh, lord, I didn't know! And you doing all that work and all!'

'Women aren't frail plants, you know, Hannah,' replied Rachel, swinging her legs to the ground. 'I've quite a strong constitution. But I get tired easily, that's all.'

'I see.' Hannah disappeared quickly as the kettle began to sing, and she returned a few moments later with a tray of tea which she set on the table beside Rachel.

'Join me,' said Rachel, indicating the seat opposite. 'I suppose I've aroused either your disapproval or your curiosity.'

Hannah gave an exclamation. 'Don't be silly, Rachel,' she exclaimed. 'What's there to disapprove of? You're married, aren't you?'

Rachel sighed. 'Yes, I am. But my husband doesn't know I'm pregnant.'

Hannah flushed. 'Oh, I see. It's not his child.'

'Yes, it is.' Rachel sighed again. 'Oh, Hannah, I can't explain, but André—my husband, that is—doesn't love me. He—he wants a divorce.'

'The pig!' Hannah was vehement. 'Leaving you in the lurch like this!'

'It's not quite like that,' Rachel had to admit. 'André would consider it a matter of principle to take care of both me and the baby if he knew. Indeed, I'm sure he would give up all thoughts of a divorce. But I don't want him that way, can you see? If—if he really loved me, it would be different. Then I would tell him. But he doesn't. He—he did some terrible things, things that left me in no doubt as to his feelings for me.' She

174

bit her lip, controlling herself with difficulty.

Hannah shook her head. 'How awful for you! But how will you manage? The shop and all?'

Rachel shrugged. 'That's why I've been out. I went to see my solicitor to ask him whether I ought to sell it.'

'I see.' Hannah nodded, looking round regretfully. 'It'll be a pity to sell it now, after you've got it so nice. It's a nice little business. It could be much better. If you had someone, someone like John, who knew a bit about antiques....'

'Does John know about antiques?'

'Some. He used to come in here when your father was alive and talk to him, but I don't suppose you noticed.'

Rachel shook her head. 'Not really, although now you mention it, I vaguely recall there was a boy...' She shrugged. 'Perhaps I shouldn't sell after all. I could always leave you and John in charge while I have the baby.'

Hannah laughed. 'We'll be married by then,' she said consideringly. 'Maybe it's not such a crazy idea.'

Rachel shook her head. 'It's no good, Hannah, I'm going to have to sell. I couldn't possibly afford to pay you to look after the shop, and in any case, I'm going to be useless in about three months' time.'

Hannah sighed. 'I suppose you're right. One day John and I are going to have a shop of our own though. It's what we both want, and Dad says he'll help us.'

Rachel nodded. 'I suppose it is nice, having a family business,' she remarked slowly. 'It's just when it develops into a corporation it becomes something else again.' But Hannah did not know to what she was referring.

Mr. Cropper finally decided it might be the best thing for Rachel to sell, and the shop was duly assessed by an estate agent, and put up for sale. Rachel thought that the sooner the deal was accomplished the better. She wanted to make other arrangements long before the baby was born.

She had several people come to see the place and all wanted possession of the flat along with the shop. She supposed it was only to be expected. After all, in these days it was safer to live on the premises. Of course, she had quite a few couples come simply out of curiosity, and she grew tired of showing people round who had absolutely no intention of buying but were merely amusing themselves at her expense. She had to watch the articles in the shop, too. People were not averse to helping themselves.

But finally a buyer, an interested buyer, came along, and after some haggling with the estate agent, he settled on a price. Rachel was forced to accept at last that she was really leaving the neighbourhood. However, Mrs. Verity had offered her temporary accommodation once the sale went through, so she was not alarmed about not yet having a place of her own. All the same, it would be a wrench to leave.

One evening, she was just getting out of the bath when she heard someone hammering on the outer door of the shop. With an exasperated exclamation she glanced at her watch. It was after nine o'clock and it was a filthy night, for it had been raining since early evening. It was the kind of English summer weather that sent holidaymakers abroad, and she couldn't imagine who could be calling at a time like this. Deciding it must be someone to look around who was not yet aware that the place had been sold, she ignored the hammering, and reached for her dressing-gown. It was made of heavy silk in a dark shade of blue, and she tied the cord securely about her thickening waist. Then she emerged into her living-room and started to comb her hair.

The hammering ceased and she breathed a sigh of relief. Whoever had called had obviously gone away in defeat. But moments later the banging started again, and Rachel felt the faintest stirrings of alarm. Surely no one would knock like that at this time of the evening. Was it possibly teenagers causing trouble?

Her fingers lingered near the telephone. Should she call the Veritys and have them investigate for her? Or should she go down and find out for herself? She hesitated. She could go down in the dark. The lights from the street outside provided sufficient illumination.

With determination, she opened the living-room door and emerged on to the landing above the shop. She could see a man's silhouette by the panels of the door, and she trembled a little. Whoever it was had stopped banging, but was still waiting, sheltering under the canopy of the doorway. Rachel bit her lip. How dared he come here at this time of night, whoever he was, disturbing her like this? Were he the new owner himself, he still had no right to arrive without first warning her.

She hovered uncertainly at the top of the stairs, and then, as she was about to turn and go back into the living-room, the man pushed open the letter box and shouted: 'Rachel! Open this door! I know you're in there! For God's sake, I'm soaking!'

Rachel swayed disbelievingly. It was André's voice. But it couldn't be André, she told herself incredulously. Not here, not in London.

She took two steps down the staircase, and then stopped again. The silhouette could be André's, and certainly the determination was André's.

With trembling steps she reached the foot of the stairs, and crossed the shop to the door. She had to step round the articles of furniture which were heaped rather haphazardly to one side, but at last she was near the panels.

'André?' she murmured, in a husky voice. 'Is that you?'

The letterbox banged impatiently. 'Of course it's me,' he said loudly. 'Open the door!'

Rachel's fingers went to the bolts, and then stopped. 'Why—why are you here?' she asked unsteadily.

She heard his angry ejaculation. 'Rachel,' he said, in a low piercing tone, 'I am attracting a great deal of attention out here. Do you want to have me arrested for trying to break in?'

Rachel compressed her lips, and with a sigh she withdrew the bolts and turned the key. André turned the handle, and the door swung inwards. Rachel stepped back, and watched him as he closed the door.

He was dressed in a dark suit and overcoat, and his hair glistened with the drops of rain upon it. He quickly removed the wet overcoat and threw it over a nearby chair.

'Well?' he said harshly. 'Aren't you going to invite me upstairs? I didn't fly all this way just to talk to you in a shadowed shop doorway.'

Rachel shrugged indifferently, but she led the way

upstairs without saying a word. In the living-room, illuminated by a standard lamp, she faced him. Going up the stairs she had mentally armed herself against what was to come, but she was unsure how strong she really could be. Why was he here? Was he in London on business? Did he think he could spend the night here? If so he was mistaken. He would never make a fool of her again.

'Well, André,' she said uncompromisingly, 'this is a surprise!'

André regarded her sombrely. 'Is it? Didn't you know I would come as soon as I could?' His expression was harsh in the lamplight. 'Haven't I always?'

Rachel pressed a hand to her throat. 'I don't know why you should,' she said tensely.

'Don't you?' André lifted his shoulders wearily. 'Maybe because I always was a fool where you were concerned!'

Rachel frowned. 'André, you're not making sense,' she said uneasily.

André looked at her intently. 'Am I not? Why didn't you come to Veros after you left Juanastra?'

'To—Veros?'

'Of course. If not for my sake then for my mother's.'

Rachel sank down on to a chair. Her legs felt weak. 'Why should I go back to Veros?' she asked unsteadily. 'My home is here.'

A muscle worked in André's cheek. 'It was the least you could do, I would have thought,' he said roughly.

Rachel shook her head. 'But why? Surely your mother knew I intended to return to London. Marcus must have told her.'

'He did. He said you were leaving Juanastra. That

was why Irena agreed to go to be with Olivia.'

'Yes?' Rachel frowned. 'So?'

André studied her face. Then he shook his head. 'You look so innocent,' he muttered. 'Maybe that's why I can't get you out of my mind!'

Rachel's heart fluttered. 'André,' she exclaimed, 'what are you talking about?'

André chewed his lip. 'All right, all right,' he said. 'You know Irena invited you to Veros. My mother sent the message with her. She knew you wanted to leave Brazil, and at my request she invited you back to Veros.'

'At your request?' echoed Rachel faintly. 'Oh, André, this doesn't make sense!' In her mind's eye she saw again the cheque in Irena's hand, heard Irena's words. Pressing the palms of her hands to her ears, she said: 'I got no message, André.'

André stared at her disbelievingly, his brows drawn together in an angry frown. 'Of course you got the message. Irena told you. She told my mother you wouldn't listen to her. That you insisted on returning to England.' He raised his eyes heavenward. 'You were gone by this time, of course, and all hell was let loose!'

'What do you mean?' Rachel felt confused. 'André, please, you're not making sense!'

André stared at her for a moment longer, and then he uttered an expletive. 'All right, then,' he muttered violently, 'this is the only sense I know!' and he pulled her up into his arms, finding her startled, parted lips with his mouth.

Rachel struggled for a moment, but the warmth of his body and the passionate intensity of his mouth were too much for her and she clung to him weakly, kissing him back. His arms gathered her still closer and she felt the hardness of his body against hers as his mouth sought her throat and shoulder, pushing aside the gown and finding her warm scented flesh.

'God,' he groaned, 'Rachel, you've got to let me care for you, look after you; I need you more than life itself!' Rachel made a concerted effort and thrust him away a little so that she could look into his face. His eyes were weary, and there was a haggard expression deepening the lines by his mouth.

'What did you say?' she whispered incredulously. 'How can you say such things? Leonie——'

'Oh, to hell with Leonie,' he muttered, smoothing her hair between his fingers. 'You're the only woman I've ever loved and you know it.'

Rachel shook her head. 'You don't mean that,' she said unsteadily. 'You know what I'm like. Bad-tempered, shrewish, unwilling to be dominated!'

'Rachel, I need you. That word constitutes everything. There will be times I know when I hate you, when I want to hurt you, but in spite of that, I love you, and I've never said that to any woman but you!'

Rachel struggled out of his arms, unwilling to believe this was really happening. 'Go—go on about Irena—and your mother,' she said. 'I didn't get any message, I maintain that, but even so—it's over a month since I came back to England.'

André sighed, and trailed the fingers of one hand down her cheek. 'I know,' he muttered. 'I think every day must have taken a year off my life.'

'What do you mean?'

'When I found you had left for England, I flew to Rio to see Olivia. To find out if you had said anything to her. But when I arrived, Olivia was in hospital and it was Irena I saw—Irena I spoke to.'

'Olivia! In hospital! Why?'

André shook his head. 'She lost the baby.'

'Oh no!'

'Yes. Maria had been naughty and Irena was scolding her. Olivia came hurrying down the stairs to stop her, but she passed out halfway down, and fell. Irena sent for the doctor, but it was too late. I believe she had been ill——'

'Yes, she had. While I was there.' Rachel turned away. 'Irena!' she exclaimed bitterly. 'Poor Olivia! I wish I'd known!'

'Yes, Irena seems to have caused a lot of trouble one way and another,' said André heavily. 'However, I understand she's planning to take a trip. On my advice.' He sighed. 'That leaves us, Rachel.'

Rachel bent her head. 'You went away without saying a word,' she reminded him in a choked voice. 'And—and there was the cheque!'

'What cheque?' André caught her arm. 'What cheque?' he repeated.

Rachel looked up at him, and comprehension dawned. 'I—I'll tell you,' she whispered. 'But first—tell me why you went away.'

André pulled her to him. 'All right,' he agreed. 'I went away because I knew I had to see Leonie and free myself from her before speaking to you. It wasn't easy, placating Leonie and her parents without causing a scandal, and then immediately afterwards my mother fell ill. It was as though events were combining to keep us apart.'

'Irena knew you were breaking with Leonie I suppose,' murmured Rachel, beginning to understand fully.

'Of course. We had quite a row about it. But then, when Marcus said you were leaving Rio, I got my mother to invite you to Veros. When you didn't come I could have killed you.'

Rachel nodded slowly. Then she cupped his face in her hands. 'Irena gave me a cheque, but no message,' she said quietly. 'She said you had said to tell me that I would know what the money was for!'

'Oh God!' André pressed her face to his shoulder. 'And you believed her?'

'Why shouldn't I? The cheque had your name on it.'

André sighed. 'I sign cheques all the time,' he muttered. 'It wouldn't have been difficult for her to obtain one. She might even have forged my signature. It wouldn't be difficult, having access to my things as she does. So that was why you left so abruptly. . . .'

Rachel sighed. 'That was part of it,' she agreed softly.

'And the rest?'

Rachel shook her head, and drew back again. 'Tell me about Olivia. How is she now?'

'She's fine. A little depressed, perhaps, but Marcus took her away after it was over, and I think she's recovering now. That was why I couldn't come immediately to England. To begin with, I was so mad, I didn't intend ever seeing you again.' He half smiled. 'And by the time I cooled down, Marcus and Olivia had left for their trip to the States, and I had the Hemming deal to complete myself.'

'I see,' Rachel nodded. 'And now you're free?'

'In every respect except one,' he muttered huskily. 'Come back here, I want to make love to you.'

Rachel did not resist. There was no point any longer, and a warm feeling of being part of a family again was stealing into her heart.

She awoke in the early hours of the morning, and brushed her hair out of her eyes with a lazy hand. Then she became aware that André was awake and was lying regarding her tenderly.

'Love me?' he murmured huskily, drawing her into the circle of his arms.

Rachel nodded. 'André,' she whispered hesitantly, 'there—there's something I've got to tell you.'

André frowned. 'Nothing bad, I hope,' he said, tracing the outline of her mouth with a lazy finger.

'I hope you won't think so,' she replied, struggling into a sitting position. 'I'm going to have a baby!'

André sat up and stared at her incredulously. 'A baby?' he repeated softly.

Rachel nodded.

'My child.' It was a statement.

'Of course.'

'And you weren't going to tell me?' he exclaimed, pain in his eyes.

Rachel put her hands on his shoulders, smoothing his brown skin with her palms. 'How could I?' she asked appealingly. 'I thought you were going to marry Leonie as soon as you were free. Had I told you about the baby then you might have thought I was asserting my rights.'

'Your *rights!*' groaned André, caressing her fingers

with his lips. 'Rachel, what can I say?'

She looked anxiously at him. 'You're not sorry?'

'Me? Sorry?' he ejaculated, shaking his head. 'Dear God, Rachel, what a question! But you—do *you* want it?'

'Oh *yes!*' Rachel was eager. 'Very much.'

André's eyes darkened. 'Our child,' he murmured wonderingly, drawing her down to him, his hands on her waist. 'Rachel, I adore you.'

'I'm going to look terrible in a few weeks,' she volunteered reluctantly.

'Not to me,' he denied, rather thickly. 'Never to me!'

André swung the tiller and the yacht curved gracefully through the channel into the lagoon. Swiftly he dismantled the sail, and Rachel steered the craft across the lake towards the landing stage.

As they neared the jetty, André dropped down into the stern beside his wife and regarded her flushed face with some amusement.

'Well?' he said lazily. 'I wouldn't exactly say you were ready for a solo voyage round Cape Horn, but you're improving!'

Rachel cast him a laughing glance. 'Praise from the master is praise indeed!' she remarked. Then she sighed. 'Oh, André, I am enjoying this! It's so long since we sailed together.'

'Hmm!' André gave her a speculative glance. 'Too long. However, I intend to remedy that in the future.'

Rachel leant forward and kissed his cheek. 'You wouldn't have wanted me to take any chances with our son, would you?' she murmured.

'Oh no!' André shook his head, soberly. 'Or with you,' he added gently. 'You are infinitely precious to me!'

Rachel's eyes were tender. 'I don't know why I deserve to be so happy,' she reflected softly. 'I haven't had much chance to talk to you since Robert was born with your mother being around and so on, but I just want you to know that I realise what a fool I was to leave you....'

André shook his head and drew her into the circle of his arm. 'I should never have let you go—should never have acted as I did! I guess we all learn by our mistakes. I should have looked after you as Marcus looked after Olivia when she lost her baby, not blown my top as I did.'

Rachel's lips touched his neck. 'I really didn't set out to lose the baby,' she said. 'You do believe that.'

André nodded, cupping her chin in his hand. 'I was a brute and an arrogant fool,' he said, tracing the line of her lips with his finger, arousing her as he was always able to do. 'But never again. And so far as the Sanchez corporation is concerned, they can find themselves a new chairman. I'll maintain an interest, of course——'

'Of course,' Rachel interrupted him mischievously.

'—but from now on my own family takes precedence.'

The yacht nudged gently against the jetty walls, and André vaulted out to secure the painter. Then he helped Rachel to join him, and they started to walk up towards the house. As they did so, Olivia came out of the house carrying Rachel's baby. At four weeks, Robert André Sanchez was small, and dark and adorable.

Rachel shook her head as they reached Olivia, and said: 'Oh, Olivia, has he been a nuisance?'

Olivia shook her head smilingly. 'Of course not. I've just been giving him his bottle, that's all, and I couldn't resist holding him for a while. Four months is such a long time to wait!'

Olivia expected another baby in four months, and this time there had been no complications.

Now they all entered the house where Marcus was busily mixing drinks. Rachel looked about her with pleasure. It was still hard to realise that she had been given a second chance, even though she knew that the love she and André shared had been strengthened by their separation. She was so lucky, so very lucky.

'Olivia tells me you've let a young couple have the shop, Rachel,' Marcus was saying now.

Rachel nodded. 'That's right. The girl, Hannah, was a great help to me when I went back to England. Her parents have the shop next door.'

'I see.' Marcus nodded. 'And do they know a lot about the business?'

'Very little,' replied André, accepting his drink. 'But they'll learn. John is a very intelligent young man. I liked him.'

'They're coming over after Christmas to spend a couple of weeks with us,' inserted Rachel. 'They hadn't a chance to take a honeymoon, so they're spending it here.'

Olivia smiled. 'I'm sure they'll love it.' She looked at her husband. 'Marcus, why can't we have a home of our own like this?'

Later, as Rachel and André were changing for dinner, Rachel said: 'Tell me honestly, André, why did

187

you come to Brazil when I was staying with Olivia and Marcus?' She turned so that he could zip up her dress, and as he did so, his hands slid down her back to her waist, tightening possessively.

'You know why,' he muttered huskily. 'I had to be sure you meant what you said that night at Veros.'

'You were so horrible to me that night,' she murmured, drawing his arms round her and leaning back against him.

'Yes, I was wasn't I?' he mouthed against her neck. 'I've told you—I hated you for what you were doing to me!'

'And now?' she asked, with some satisfaction.

'And now I've got to finish getting dressed,' he replied, rather huskily, 'or would you rather we missed dinner altogether...?'

Romance
is
Beautiful

Get to the
HEART OF
HARLEQUIN

HARLEQUIN READER SERVICE is your passport to The Heart of Harlequin . . .

if You...

♥   enjoy the mystery and adventure that comes from the world's leading publisher of romantic novels . . .

♥   want to keep up-to-date on all of our new releases, eight brand new Romances and four Harlequin Presents, each month . . .

♥   are interested in valuable reissues of best-selling back titles . . .

♥   are intrigued by exciting, money-saving jumbo volumes . . .

♥   would like to enjoy North America's unique monthly magazine, "Harlequin" — available **ONLY** through Harlequin Reader Service . . .

♥   are excited by **anything new** under the Harlequin sun.

then...

YOU should be on the Harlequin Reader Service **INFORMATION PLEASE** list — it costs you nothing to receive our news bulletins and intriguing brochures. Please turn page for news of an **EXCITING FREE OFFER.**

a Special Offer for You...

Just by requesting information about Harlequin Reader Service, we will send you, with absolutely no obligation, a newly designed, special "limited edition" copy of **VIOLET WINSPEAR**'s first Harlequin bestseller

LUCIFER'S ANGEL

You will be fascinated by this explosive story of the fast-moving, hard-living world of Hollywood in the '50s. An unforgettable tale of an innocent young woman who meets and marries a dynamic but ruthless movie producer, this gripping novel combines excitement, intrigue, mystery and romance.

A complimentary copy is waiting for YOU — just fill out the coupon on the next page and send it to us today.

Don't Miss...

any of the exciting details of Harlequin Reader Service **COLLECTOR'S YEAR**

♥ It promises to be one of the greatest publishing events in our history and we're certain you'll want to be a part of it.

♥ Learn all about this great new series.

♥ These reissues are of some of the earliest and best-selling Harlequin Romances.

♥ Each is presented with a new, exciting and distinctive cover design.

To become a part of the Harlequin Reader Service **INFORMATION PLEASE** list, and to learn more about **COLLECTOR'S YEAR** — simply fill in the coupon below and you will also receive LUCIFER'S ANGEL by Violet Winspear.

SEND TO: ➡

Harlequin Reader Service,
"Information Please",
M.P.O. Box 707,
Niagara Falls, New York 14302.

CANADIAN RESIDENTS ➡

Harlequin Reader Service,
Stratford, Ont., Can.   N5A 6W4

Name _____

Address _____

City _____ State/Prov. _____

Zip/Postal Code _____

IP 306